THE ALVIN GOODFELLOW CASE FILES

FILES

VOLUME ONE

LEAH R CUTTER

KNOTTED ROAD PRESS

The Alvin Goodfellow Case Files
Volume One

Published by Knotted Road Press
www.KnottedRoadPress.com

ISBN:

Cover Art:

ID 70610496 © Helen Vonallmen | Dreamstime.com
ID 108618231 © Ryan Paul Ragnini | Dreamstime.com
ID 50546250 © Valeriy Kachaev | Dreamstime.com
ID 91040948 © Rafael Torres Castaño | Dreamstime.com
ID 111009911 © Valeriy Kachaev | Dreamstime.com

Cover and interior design copyright © 2020 Knotted Road Press
http://www.KnottedRoadPress.com

The Case of the Missing Mogul first published in *Boundary Shock Quarterly*, Issue #6, "Ray Guns and Space Babes"

The Case of the Vanishing Cream first published in *I Like My Science Mad*

The Case of the Missing Twin first published in Boundary Shock Quarterly, Issue #10, "Homofuturis"

The Case of the Bungled Bank Robbery first published in *Nuns with Guns*

Reviews
It's true. Reviews help me sell more books. If you've enjoyed this story, please consider leaving a review of it on your favorite site.

Come someplace new...
Are you a traveler? Do you enjoy exploring strange new worlds, new cultures, new people?

Journey into the various lands envisioned by Leah Cutter.

Sign up for my newsletter and I'll start you on your travels with a free copy of my book, *The Island Sampler*.

I will never spam you or use your email for nefarious purposes. You can also unsubscribe at any time.

http://www.LeahCutter.com/newsletter/

ALSO BY LEAH R CUTTER

Mysteries

The Purloined Letter Opener

The Rabbit Mysteries

The Shredded Veil Mysteries

The Halley Brown Mysteries

Dancer in Darkness

Trophy Hunters

The Cassie Stories

Poisoned Pearls

Tainted Waters

Spoiled Harvest

Bloodied Ice

The Witch's Progress

Circle of Air

Circle of Water

Circle of Fire

Circle of Earth

Seattle Trolls

The Changeling Troll

The Princess Troll

The Fairy-Bridge Troll

The Troll-Demon War

The Troll-Human War

The Troll-Troll War

Forgotten Gods

A Wind Blown Torment

A Stone Strewn Clash

A Sea Washed Victory

Tanish Empire Trilogy

The Glass Magician

The Desert Heart

The Ghost Dog

The Shadow Wars Trilogy

The Raven and the Dancing Tiger

The Guardian Hound

War Among the Crocodiles

The Chronicles of Franklin

Franklin Versus The Popcorn Thief

Franklin Versus The Soul Thief

Franklin Versus The Child Thief

Huli Intergalactic - Science/Space Fantasy

Origins

The Strawberry Girl

[1]

THE CASE OF THE MISSING MOGUL

IT STARTED ON A TUESDAY. I WAS SITTING IN MY OFFICE with my feet up on my desk, congratulating myself on a job well done. I'd even taken a sharp hit from the bottle of whiskey in the bottom right-hand drawer and was considering taking another, as well as the afternoon off.

You'd think with a moniker like Alvin Goodfellow, Private Investigator, that I would have known better. Hell, I'd even run ads on the radio proclaiming me as the PI to the stars, one of the good guys, the best you could hire on the Moon, Venus, or Mars.

But temptation comes in many different forms, including a sweet-smelling alien babe just waiting to trip up the unwary.

The fan overhead turned lazily, not doing much to freshen up the stale air piped in from Central. I had a water cooler in one corner, burbling to itself, a comforting sound. In the opposite corner I had three dinged up, second-hand, black-metal file cabinets that contained the notes from my cases. I kept them locked to dissuade casual violations of my clients' privacy, as anyone determined enough and armed with a paperclip could probably break in.

Despite the ads, I only had a single office on the Moon. It was located in the section of the Stockton Warrens known as the Fishbowl. Some idiot at Central had decided that all the windows on the buildings in this section were to be convex, bowing out into the corridors, as much as two feet in places. Supposed to give us poor mooks the impression of having more space than we actually did, instead of feeling closed in and claustrophobic most of the time.

Plus, the stupid windows just created congestion whenever a shift was over and the hallways got crowded, workers expanding and contracting in pulses as they passed by windows in their way home.

So I kept the shades drawn and the lights up high. Wasn't as if I had any sort of view except the corridor outside. My offices were underground, of course. Some of the newer colonies had fancy domes covering them, but I wasn't sure I trusted even the NuGlass that much. Better to be in a warren with automatic, built-in airlocks at regular intervals in case there was a breach.

My future looked rosy at that point, expenses paid for the next month, which meant I wasn't going to have to immediately go searching for a new client. I'd just finished a job for Mrs. B—, or rather, the soon to be ex- Mrs. B—. I'd gotten paid handsomely for this one. (I try not to take on charity cases, but I've always been a sucker for a sob story from a pretty dame.)

Seemed that Mrs. B— had suspicions that her husband might have been cheating on her with his secretary at the bank. Turned out she was right, though she hadn't known the half of it.

Mr. B— had been cheating on her with his secretary. As

well as one of the tellers. And a schoolmarm who lived two corridors away.

Not sure what they saw in the guy. Pudgy older man with gray hair and a pasty white face who dressed in double-breasted suits that weren't doing him any favors. Maybe he'd been stringing them all along, promising to make them the new Mrs. B——. They'd get their chance, shortly.

The photos I took of the man and his various mistresses would stand up in court, and Mrs. B—— had a slew of them, clutched in her grasping hand as she exited triumphantly from my office.

I was just reaching for the bottle again, planning to close up early for the day, when *she* came strolling in.

She had gorgeous white hair that looked soft and sleek, like the finest silk. It set off her dark green skin nicely. Her eyes were amber, like good whiskey, while her lips were redder than fresh cherries, just waiting to be tasted.

She wore an elegant sheath dress, pale green, the style made popular by the Moon's First Lady. However, this wasn't a shapeless piece of clothing, no, it clung in all the right places, showing off her great rack as well as the curves of her hips.

Around her neck she had a set of pearls that were each the size of a baby's fist, probably mined from the hidden oceans of Mars. She also wore a stole made of what looked like faded fox fur. (I learned later it had come from Jupiter and one of the creatures who lived on the winds there.)

I stood up, glad that I'd already taken my feet off my desk, buttoning my jacket quickly so I'd at least appear to be somewhat respectable. There wasn't anything I could do about my ginger hair. I kept it cut short so it wouldn't curl too much. And I'd been told that my blue eyes changed with my emotions, going from soft to sharp. I had freckles that never faded, as well as what had been called a baby face, which I used ruthlessly to my advantage when I needed someone to believe I was more innocent than I appeared.

The job kept me fit enough, all the walking and bad hours, living on the edge of my budget so I rarely had the opportunity to overindulge my stomach. If I ever gave the business up, I'd have to start doing something healthy, like maybe dancing.

"Hello," I said, happily watching the dame slink across the floor of my office and come to stand behind one of the guest chairs. "What can I help you with?"

She bit her lip for a moment before she replied.

That was disturbing, I had to admit. Women from Venus all had very white, very sharp, pointed teeth. Of course, some men were desperate enough to overlook that considering all the other assets these women possessed.

"My husband is missing," she said in a voice that matched the rest of her, smoky and rich, the words sliding easily through the still air. "I'm afraid there's been foul play."

"Why don't you tell me about it, Mrs....?" I said, gesturing toward the guest chair she stood behind.

She still hesitated. "The reason I'm coming to see you and not the police is because my husband's business isn't always on the right side of the law."

"I see," I said, hesitating myself.

Sure, I knew the back rooms and hallways where those sorts of deals were made. Some of the trade that went on in unofficial channels was necessary—Central occasionally tried to collect too great a piece of the pie, which quickly fueled the black market, until they came to their senses and knocked their taxes back down.

Other trades, though...I didn't want any part of them. They included unofficial domestic workers who frequently became something more akin to slaves. To say nothing of the drugs coming out of the factories hidden on the far side of the Moon, that took a man's will as well as his money.

The dame appeared to understand my hesitation. "Trust me," she said, her voice turning even silkier. "While our trade may be illegal, it isn't immoral. Nothing you would disapprove of."

"Trust you?" I laughed harshly. I had to let her know where she stood. "Listen, lady. I don't even trust my own mother when it comes to these sorts of things." Didn't help that Mom sat wasting away in a home, addicted to pain killers that some quack had prescribed for her years ago.

However, that response appeared to mollify the dame. "Good," she said, sliding down into the chair. "I can work with someone willing to give me that level of honesty."

I sat myself, pulling the legal pad I kept on the desk for notes, along with a fresh pen.

"So tell me about your husband," I said, hand poised.

She bit her lip again. That fresh reminder that no matter how Human or gorgeous she looked, no matter how much her sweet perfume might remind one of the (rare) scheduled rain in one of the (rarer) parks, she was an alien.

"You'll keep your notes private?" she asked, her eyes darting to the file cabinets behind me.

"Always," I solemnly promised her.

"Then let me tell you my story."

"You can call me Carol," she said as she sat back in her chair, making herself more comfortable.

I don't think it was that calculated a move, though she did wiggle in the most interesting way as she got settled, her breasts jiggling just the perfect amount to make sure that she had my undivided attention.

"My real, Venusian name, well, it's difficult for Humans to say," she admitted.

I wasn't surprised by that. It was one of the reasons why Humans were sometimes foolish enough to look beyond the pointed teeth—it was rumored that Venusian women (and men) had very talented tongues.

"My husband is Richard Wagner," she said, pronouncing the "W" as a "V". She slid a small black-and-white photo across the desk. It showed a man in his mid-forties, white, healthy and prosperous. Reminded me a little of the pudgy banker I'd just been following, though Wagner was less flabby, better dressed, and probably had better hygiene.

However, that gave me pause right there. "He's Human?" I asked pointedly, wanting to make sure I was seeing things clearly.

"He is." She gave a little sigh, and another whiff of her lovely, rain-like perfume cascaded over me. "Ours was a love match. The money came later."

I doubted that very much. Venusians had a reputation of being gold diggers, both the men and the women. Chances were, Carol had decided that she was in love with Richard Wagner only *after* she'd seen his bank account.

"What does your husband do?" I said.

"We own a shipping company. We started off small, just a single ship, running goods from Venus to the Moon and back," she said.

I kept my head down, taking notes and not saying anything. Starting "small" with "just" a ship meant that they'd begun with a sizable chunk of credits. More than I'd make in five years or so. Ships weren't cheap, no matter what the ads would have you believe. Even if they'd hocked themselves up to their necks, the down payment alone was far beyond the common worker.

Yup. A "love" match all right, particularly if the ship had been Richard's and Carol had started out much poorer than she appeared today.

"Then, we got lucky," Carol said. "You remember the shortage of air filters that happened six years ago?"

I nodded. "Mold or something found in the factory, right?" I said. The air filters were spreading toxins that caused all sorts of exotic side effects, including creating some mutants who supposedly still lived deep under the warrens of the Moon.

"We'd just stocked up on a fresh supply of exactly that type of filter," Carol said, "and were already en route when the call went out."

Lucky indeed. That wasn't the sort of luck that could be manufactured.

"Central paid double the normal rate," Carol purred, still sounding very satisfied with herself.

I didn't like it, personally, making a killing off other people's suffering. Without air, the entire city would have died.

However, I wasn't one to talk, as most of my clients were miserable and needed my help to make others more miserable than they were.

"With that modest investment, we were able to buy another ship, expand our business, ship even more goods from Venus. Then we got even more lucky."

The sultry seducer gave me an honest, happy smile. It was good to know there was a soul somewhere underneath all the trappings, after all.

"We found a supply of Golden Eggs," she said.

Carol had judged me correctly. Golden Eggs, mined in caves found below the jungles of Venus, produced a mild hallucinogen and gave Humans a brief sense of euphoria. As far as I understood the drug, you crushed the egg in your palm, then inhaled the gas. It wasn't addictive, at least not as far as the scientists could tell. However, as it was out of Central's control (couldn't be replicated by their own chemists) they decided to declare the eggs illegal pending review.

That review had been going on for a few years, now. Probably the smugglers had been bribing the right people at Central so they could keep making an illegal, untaxable profit.

"After the first delivery, well, it was easy to set up a larger corporation, add ships," Carol said. "The majority of our business is still legitimate," she emphasized. "Only a small portion, maybe one shipment in ten, contains any eggs. And they are never the entire shipment."

"Was your husband actually flying with one of the shipments?" I asked, surprised. Wouldn't a corporate mogul stick to his desk and his three-martini business lunches instead of grunt work?

That earned me a proud smile. "Richard believed in keeping the captains on their toes. About once a month he'd pick a random ship to fly on, making sure that everything was still being maintained to his high standards."

I didn't say anything. On the one hand, sure, random inspections were one way to keep the everyday working schmuck in line.

On the other hand, in my line of business, regular trips away from the wife, particularly off world, generally meant that something else—something shady—was going on.

"Richard always calls me when he arrives," Carol continued. "Which he did, this time. He also calls me just before he leaves, with a couple of calls in between. He'd only been planning on staying two days. But he never called that final time. And when I tried to find him, when I phoned his hotel, I couldn't reach him. The hotel said he never checked out. They went into his room and found all his things were there, already packed and ready to go."

"How many days ago was this?" I asked. That was one of the problems with spaceflight. While phones worked instantaneously, the signals broadcasting out of the huge towers located on top of Epsilon Peak, ships themselves still took days or weeks to reach their destination.

"He came here sixteen days ago," Carol replied. "Which means that his trip should have ended fourteen days ago. I know, I know! I kept hoping that he'd call. I made so many excuses for him. Told myself that he'd just been delayed. I didn't leave the house, waiting for that phone to ring. But the call never came."

I gave a grim nod. Sixteen days, or even fourteen, didn't create the coldest trail that I'd ever had for the start of a case, but it was damned close.

"What hotel was he staying at?" I asked. "And do you still have the room booked?"

She shook her head. "The Piedmont, downtown. I don't have the room anymore. The hotel had to move his things into storage three days ago. They were booked solid and didn't want to hold the room open, even though I offered them double the going rate."

More likely they didn't want to be forced to cooperate with the kind of investigation that would occur when a prominent businessman went missing, keeping the room off the market and unavailable for days or even weeks while science geeks with their sniffers and fancy powders went over the room looking for fingerprints as well as any traces of blood.

"Have you collected his bags from storage?"

"I did. This morning," she said. "There wasn't anything in

them that I didn't expect. Everything had been repacked neatly, as if he was getting ready to go."

I wasn't about to take her word on that. If he was seeing someone on the Moon, and he was smart, the sort of memorabilia generated by an affair should be kept in a locker or an office here, never carried back to the where the wife was.

Most men weren't that smart.

"I'd like to look through his bags," I told her. Chances were, I'd find something that didn't actually belong.

"I'll have them delivered tomorrow," she assured me.

"Would you happen to know the names of the people he was dealing with? The ones he supplied?"

She reeled off the names of two individuals who I'd never heard of before, along with Jimmy the Skunk.

Jimmy wasn't named that because of his smell—small, closed-in places like moon warrens weren't the place for individuals who didn't pay attention to their hygiene.

What Jimmy did have was black hair that had started coming in pure white. While Jimmy wasn't necessarily smelly, he was lazy, so he'd frequently end up with a large white streak down the center part of his otherwise midnight-black dyed hair.

I knew of Jimmy, though I'd never worked with him or shaken him down. He was a small-time crook who ran confidence games out of the back rooms of illegal gambling joints. He wasn't a dealer or a fence. As far as I knew, he wasn't an official informant for the cops. Still, word in the street was that he'd squeal quick enough to anyone if they put the squeeze on him.

What was the upright Richard Wagner doing with a petty criminal like that?

Maybe I had an idea of where to start this case, despite how cold it seemed.

Carol agreed to triple my normal fee without blinking an eye, paying me for two days' work up front. She also agreed to pay normal expenses, as long as they were itemized.

Made me wonder if I should have charged more.

She told me that she'd have Richard's bag delivered tomorrow morning, early. And insisted that I was to call her as soon as I had news, any news at all.

I easily promised the dame that, though I knew I'd be calling only when I was damned good and ready.

I looked over my notes after she'd left. Something wasn't right. The entire case just had that stench to it, Jimmy the Skunk notwithstanding.

First of all, the Piedmont was in Lunar Central, the heart of downtown. Jimmy operated on the strip, which was pretty far west of the hotel. There were a lot of places that offered the same sort of entertainment much closer to downtown.

Plus, I initially assumed that the Wagner Corporation warehouses were located with the rest of the business district in the east, almost as far away from the hotel as the strip, though in the opposite direction.

I closed my eyes, breathing in that sweet wet scent that Carol had left behind, while I tried to concentrate and bring up a map of the city in my head. I finally gave in and rummaged in my center drawer for my old paper copy, as well as a battered yellow-pages directory of businesses.

Seemed I was wrong. The Wagner Corporation warehouses and business offices were just off the new Lunar Parkway district. If I put the hotel as the center, starting point, that put the strip at two o'clock, while the warehouses were actually directly at noon. That gave me an interesting pie shape to work with, as chances were, Richard Wagner's business was actually conducted in that area.

First stop for me was the hotel, to see if there were any clues left on that cold trail.

I doubted that my luck would be that good, though.

THE PIEDMONT HAD BEEN BUILT TO EARTH-SCALE, meaning that instead of a closed, cramped lobby like what I had at my apartment building, it extended up two full floors. Windows lit up the space, full of fake daylight as no sun could ever shine through them. Black and white tile made up the unyielding floor and broke the many conversations into hard, chipped sounds. Bellboys in red and gold uniforms with box hats and white gloves lounged beside their golden cages to the right of the door, waiting for that next big tip. A huge concierge desk stood just to the left, commanded by an older gentleman with a blue uniform and silver hair, the sergeant major ordering around the rest of the staff.

Right in front of me, opposite the grand doors, stood the long reception desk, staffed by Humans and Venusians, as well as a tall female warrior from Mars. They looked friendly enough, but I knew they'd all thumb their noses at me if I approached them. I did wear a nice enough brown suit with a stylish brown fedora. However, my shoes were plain, not fancy Italian leather, and my teeth, while nice enough, had never been straightened or polished like theirs.

So instead of going to the desk, I walked into the joint like I belonged there, then straight around the corner, toward the elevators in the back. A house phone had been tucked into a little alcove right beside the tall brass doors.

As I had figured, the phone could only be used for calling rooms in the hotel. I dialed the operator, and had her put me in touch with housekeeping.

"Uhm, hi," I said when a Mrs. Ellison, head of housekeeping, answered the phone. "I don't know if I've reached the right department or if you can help me or not," I said, rushing the words and sounding completely unsure of myself. "My boss was here, at the Piedmont, Mr. Wagner. Room 1233. He left without checking out. Now his wife is here, flown over from Venus, and she's insisting that there's a bag missing."

"May I assure you there is no bag missing," Mrs. Ellison said frostily. "You should check with security—"

"I know, I know," I said. "And they're going to give me the runaround. I was just hoping you might not? Is the room empty? Could I take a quick look around? That way I can assure Mrs. Wagner that you people are top notch, on the up and up. Please?"

There was a pause while Mrs. Ellison considered my request.

"It would sure mean the world to me," I assured her eagerly. "And Mrs. Wagner is always very generous."

"Very well," she said, probably calculating the size of the tip I would give her. "I'll meet you on the twelfth floor directly."

"That's so swell," I told her. "Thank you very much."

I waited for the elevator to come down to the lobby, mingling with the much fancier dressed guests. The amount of perfume surprised me. Or maybe that was just the scent of credits. I kept my hat down over my eyes so that no one could get a good look at my face.

The elevator operator was an older woman with iron-colored hair and a face like a hawk who sat beside the door. She was dressed like the concierge, in a blue uniform with white gloves. Her voice sounded as though she had a three-pack-a-day habit as she asked the guests their floors.

Instead of being one of the more modern lifts with buttons you could push yourself, she sat beside an old-fashioned lever that was used to steer you to the proper floor.

It had an ivory handle and the floor numbers were all embossed on a half circle, in polished brass.

Generally, you had to have a feel for that sort of lever. It wasn't automatic, and so you really needed the attendant to operate it. Plus, it was a handy way to hide floors in the spaces between the number, with most of the guests being clueless about the private areas.

I would bet that Mrs. Wagner hadn't realized that such a thing was possible, that her husband was staying in a hotel that probably doubled as a casino most nights. The perfume made more sense now if there were burlesque dancers on the in-between floors who revealed more than the law generally allowed. What I'd smelled was the first shift of girls going to work.

I'd have to poke around and see if anyone could get me an invite.

The twelfth floor turned out to be in rarified air, the top of the joint. At least I wasn't the only one getting off there, so I didn't have to make nice with the hatchet lady driving the elevator.

Mrs. Ellison waited for me next to the door to the room. I figure she got there more quickly on a staff elevator. She wore a prim beige dress, complete with a starched white apron, collar, and cuffs. Given the stiffness of her outfit, it was obvious that she was in charge of ordering the maids around, and never stooped to doing the work herself.

I pushed my hat onto the back of my head and gave her a great, goofy grin. "Thanks ever so much for this," I told her as I came up. "This is really swell."

She gave me a quick appraisal then dismissed me as a nobody, which had been my intent. She had a large ring of keys on a slender silver chain, attached to her belt, which she unhooked and then started searching for the right one.

I was impressed. Normally, the staff in a place like this

had skeleton keys to open the rooms. Seemed that the guests here valued their privacy more, and so each floor had its own separate master key. Good to know if I ever needed to break in on some future case.

Mrs. Ellison opened the door and gestured for me to go in.

I could have fit three of my offices in the grand living room. The furniture was dark and well maintained, with a leather couch and three large matching wing-backed chairs around a central low table, perfect for casual meetings. Pictures of bright landscapes hung on the far wall, to give the impression of looking outside. Even a moonscape hung there.

To the right stood a wet bar with the alcohol decanted into shiny crystal bottles. In a cheaper joint, it would be no-name rotgut, but I bet that here, all of that lovely liquor was top shelf.

To the left stood two open doors, one to the bedroom and another to the ensuite bathroom.

Faux wood made up the floors, as even a place as fancy as this probably couldn't afford wood shipped up from Earth. But it was really high quality. The floors even had that bounce that generally you only got with wood.

I walked immediately to the couch, and slid my hand between the arm and the cushion, as if hunting for loose pocket change.

Took an effort to keep a straight face when my fingers found a folded piece of paper tucked away there.

I palmed it, then industriously searched the other side. After that, I made a show of looking in the closet in the bedroom, searching the top of the shelf above the hangers, then I looked around the bathroom.

Finally, I turned and gave Mrs. Ellison a sheepish grin.

"Seems Mrs. Wagner was mistaken. I can go and reassure her that this sure is one swell place."

Mrs. Ellison just stood there, unmoving, with one hand slightly open on her thigh.

"Oh, oh! Right!" I said. I fumbled for my wallet, sliding away the found paper and slipping out a larger bill than the housekeeper deserved. "And we can keep this just between you and me, right?" I asked as I handed it over to her.

"Your privacy is assured here," Mrs. Ellison said as she quickly put the bribe in her apron pocket.

"Thanks ever so much," I told her again as I quickly exited the room.

Possibly the paper had nothing to do with Mr. Wagner and his disappearance. I couldn't allow myself to hope.

Still, I kept that goofy, silly grin on my face for probably much longer than necessary.

———

I STOPPED AT A LITTLE COFFEE SHOP TUCKED AWAY OFF the main tunnel, a place where the maids and other local workers would go and not the rich folks who would shop downtown.

A case with pastries and a few lonely donuts sat next to the old-fashioned register at the end of the long counter. The air smelled of toasted bread and burnt coffee. Seemed in the morning they'd also do eggs on the tiny burner just behind the counter, though the sign on the wall did warn that they'd only serve until they ran out.

A table with two chairs was located under the window looking out on the corridor, already occupied by two students who had books scattered across it, along with papers covered in equations and fancy slide rules. The only other seats were along the counter, three of which were filled with old retirees reading their daily news.

A cup of joe here was more expensive than at the joints I regularly frequented. That amount of credits should have gotten me a Danish as well. Maybe some butter. At least the coffee tasted pretty good. I didn't grumble much as I took it down to the end of the counter, away from everyone else for a modicum of privacy.

After making sure that all the other customers in the joint appeared to be paying attention to their own petty lives, I fished out the folded piece of paper from my wallet.

Written in pencil, in block letters, was a single word.

Fondue.

What the heck did that mean? Was it a new drug that I'd never heard of before? A new dance move? What kind of hinky stuff had Richard Wagner been getting into?

I reeled myself back from all the flights of fancy that my brain was racing along, making myself remember something Old Dick had told me when I was still wet behind the ears.

KISS

Keep it simple, stupid.

I'd suspected earlier that the hotel had "extra" floors to it, and that you'd need to slip the elevator attendant a large tip as well as know the password to gain access.

Looked as though I might just have found my way into that party.

AS THERE WERE STILL SEVERAL HOURS OF BRIGHT LIGHTS to burn, I figured I'd go pay a call on Jimmy the Skunk before heading back to the Piedmont. I stayed at the coffee shop for a while, giving in and paying for a serving of toast. While the bread was almost blackened on one side and still white on the other, at least the jam they served was delicious, an orange marmalade that was the perfect combination of sweet and sour.

It didn't take me long to find the new place that Jimmy was operating out of. Seemed that he'd fallen on the wrong side of his previous partner and had had to move his poker game to a different back room. Jimmy was like that.

It wasn't that Central tried to illegalize all gambling. Even the bureaucrats in charge had recognized just how stupid that would be. But they had put limits on the amount you could win (or lose), trying to keep idiots from losing their shirts.

However, with their rules they'd also made most of the games as exciting as taking a walk along a corridor instead of a rollercoaster ride. Plus, the official gambling parlors all had to have their slice of the action, so the house took a lot more off the top if you did manage to win.

Only the most desperate (or the most stupid) went in for that sort of thing. It was great for tourists, or for students who wanted to have fun for the night, maybe a bachelor party.

Anyone who was serious about their cards or dice went somewhere else.

The Gin Mill looked like an ordinary dive bar out front. It had a pink neon sign of a martini glass on one side of the marquee that was constantly filling and refilling itself with bubbles, which honestly, no self-respecting gin should have. The single door in the center of the building had a gold star on it, as if to indicate here was the place for suckers. No windows of course—why bother putting them in when they'd always be closed and blocked?

I walked past the front of the building, then turned the corner and came back up the alleyway. A discreet metal door marked the back entrance. No handle on it. Not even a buzzer.

I boldly knocked, my knuckles smarting from the hard metal.

As I expected, a rough looking bouncer poked his head out at me. He had a bulldog face that probably even his mother didn't love. He towered over me. Though he was Human, he looked as big as one of the warriors from Mars, and just as muscular and tough.

"You got a game?" I asked, staring unimpressed by him. "Heard that Jimmy the Skunk operates in these parts."

That earned me a tight smile. "Just a sec."

He kept the door open and reached for some gizmo. I recognized it as a type of electronic sniffer. It had enough buttons and knobs to make even the geekiest boffin happy.

Wasn't sure exactly what he was checking for. Did they now have devices that could smell cop? Who knew what sort of wacky invention the scientists would come up with next? Hell, they were still talking about flying cars down on Earth, someday.

Whatever it was he was checking for, I seemed to pass. "Jimmy's in parlor number three," the guard said.

I reached into my pocket for the bill folded there, ready to hand him a tip. Surprised the hell out of me when he waved it away.

"Boss would have my nuts if he ever found out I was taking money on the side," the guy said. He gave me a great, tooth-filled grin, probably supposed to make me feel at ease. "Pays me well enough that I don't have to."

Huh. An honest bouncer? Don't think I'd ever met one before.

"Good to know. Thanks," I said, doffing my hat to him as I passed.

The hallway was made out of cheap NuPlastic—basically moonrock that had been crushed, added to a soup of chemicals, then hardened. I called it cheap because the stone hadn't been pulverized, so chunks of white rock still stuck out from the unyielding dark gray walls. The floor was common concrete, a lighter gray. Recessed lights pointed down from the ceiling, hard to knock out in a fight but not too bright either, giving the hallway a serious case of creepy shadows.

The doors had bright, gold numbers nailed to the center of them. Turned out there were six doors in all. I suspected that would make the front, public bar really shallow.

On the official paperwork, was the back of this place owned by a different company? Or did they make good enough money to pay the hefty bribes it would take to get the cops to look the other way?

I pushed my hat back further on my head and pasted on my goofy grin just before I opened the door to parlor number three.

The room was smaller than I'd thought it would be, probably only ten feet square. Then again, the back door hadn't been in the center of the building. The even-numbered rooms were probably twice as long as the odd-numbered ones.

A round table filled the center of the room, surrounded by chairs. Only a couple of players sat there with their cards carefully guarded, though the table could hold as many as a dozen.

Jimmy the Skunk sat directly opposite the door. Looked as though he hadn't dyed his hair in a while, as there was at least a two-inch white streak running down the center of his skull. He had more of a weasely face than I remembered, the skin sallow and the cheeks pocked. His nose was probably the sharpest thing about his appearance: His black eyes looked sleepy, as if he'd missed his long-overdue afternoon nap.

"Fifty credits to get to the table," Jimmy told me. "Opening bid is twenty."

"You serious?" complained the guy sitting to Jimmy's left. He wore merely a vest instead of a jacket, and his white shirt had seen better days. His flabby face looked red in the dim light, as if he was about to burst yet more blood cells. At one point he'd probably been a blond, based on his pale eyebrows and the fringe of hair remaining. His skull shined with sweat and he smelled desperate.

"What?" Jimmy asked.

"This game started with two hundred," the man said.

"Need more blood," Jimmy replied. He gave me a shark's grin. "Fresh blood."

If I was as naïve as I appeared, with that goofy grin of mine, that should have put me right off.

Seemed as though old Jimmy was calling my bluff.

"Fine by me," I said, still sounding as innocent as they come as I took the place with my back directly to the door, the deadman's chair. The place that only an innocent fool would take.

I knew I was sending mixed messages. I was trying to play with Jimmy's head, just as he was trying to game mine.

The other guy at the table just grunted. Unless he had no legs, he'd be a tall drink of water when he stood up, uncomfortably tall for a moon warren rat. His long face went with his lean hands. He had a soft chin and eyes that had watched too many artificial sunsets alone. He was here for the thrill, though his luck was probably worse than mine.

I waited through the rest of the ongoing hand, the tall man taking the other for a long ride. Seemed he was better at betting than the red-faced man, and bluffed his way along with three of a kind.

It was an easy way to spend the rest of the afternoon, winning some hands and losing others. The talk was loose and the whiskey that kept getting delivered to the table watered down.

The red-faced man—Joe, he turned out to be—was a sore loser. Surprising for a game like this, where the stakes weren't that high. It was obvious that Melvin, the taller man, was just here to kill some time, like me, though I was waiting for Jimmy to take a break so I could talk with him privately.

Still, after an hour or so, I managed to turn the conversation to the topic I was really interested in: where could a man get his hands on a few of the newest shipment of Golden Eggs?

Jimmy turned a sharp eye my way. I gave a long-suffering sigh. "My girl just left," I admitted, letting my grin grow sad and morose. "I just need a pick-me-up. Something to get me going again."

That actually was a legitimate use of a Golden Egg. The effect was short lived, but afterward, people did remark that they felt happier in general for a week or so.

Surprisingly, Melvin was the one who replied. "I hear ya, brother," he said. He sounded as solemn as a street corner preacher. "But I got something much better for you. You should try Dragon Eggs, instead."

I wasn't much up on the drug trade. Tried to stay as far away from it as possible. I had my whiskey and that was good enough for me.

"Never heard of those," I admitted. It actually wasn't surprising. Dealers were always coming up with new names for the same thing in an effort to stay one step ahead of the law.

Melvin gave me a wistful smile. "Same happy effect," he said. "Bit more intense. But the afterward lasts longer. Lots longer."

"I don't know," I said. "I'm just looking for a one-time thing, you know?" Talking about addiction wasn't something that even fine upstanding criminals did. I'd had too close of an experience with it, due to dear old Mom, to even start looking at that path.

Jimmy came in at that point. "Melvin's right. It's a longer afterward. But you don't got no worry about having to come see me regular-like."

As an oblique reassurance went, it was pretty good.

"How much are these Dragon Eggs going for? Compared to Golden Eggs?" I asked. I'd been betting conservatively all afternoon, complaining more than once that I wasn't made of money, stating that Central only shipped air out to the warrens, not credits.

"'Bout twice what you'd normally pay," Jimmy said. "The after-effect is also that long."

"I don't know," I said. "Let me think about it."

Soon enough, Melvin and Joe took a break, standing and stretching their legs and going to use the facilities. That left Jimmy and me alone at the table.

"I can make you a good deal on Dragon Eggs," Jimmy assured me as soon as the other two had left the room. "Better than what Melvin could give you."

"I don't know," I said, continuing to be wary. "What are Dragon Eggs?"

"They're just Golden Eggs that have been enhanced," Jimmy said. He passed me a business card that just had the letters GE on it. "On your way out, hand this to the bartender up front. He'll show you the merchandise. You don't have to buy any. But I'm not sure I'd come back here looking for another game if you don't."

"Got it," I said, slipping the card into my jacket pocket. "Thanks."

We played another hour or so before I finally cashed in. I was a couple hundred credits ahead, not counting the buy in. I tipped Jimmy well before I headed out.

Restrooms were in the main building, up front. I went up the hallway, through the door, and into a darkened room. A bouncer perched on a stool to one side, looking like the smaller sibling of the guy at the back. He wordlessly pointed to the right, in the direction of the stalls.

I took care of business then came back out, pausing on the threshold to let my eyes adjust to the dim light. On the other side of the bouncer stood a long bar. It looked like a traditional dive, with mirrors on the walls behind the two shelves with booze on them. The bar itself was made out of that same NuPlastic as the walls in the back, though the top was solid steel, dull and scratched. At least a half dozen stools were bolted to the concrete floor in front of the bar.

Cheap plastic chairs and tables were scattered across the rest of the room. They were black and showed white scars, scratches, and a lot of use. The air still smelled of the industrial cleaners used to sanitize every surface. Maybe half the tables were occupied with workers who'd knocked off their shift early, concentrating on the conversation they were having with their beer.

The bartender was a short, squat man, looking like the runt of the litter that produced the two bouncers. Completely bald with a massive beard that he wore forked and braided, like some kind of junior varsity Viking warrior. He'd made an art of polishing glasses, as if even a single speck of dust offended him.

He stayed at his end of the bar until he was good and ready to come over and wait on me. "Whatcha have?" he asked, his voice surprisingly high for such a rotund man.

"Whiskey, neat," I told him.

He reached for the bottom shelf and an unmarked bottle, having judged correctly that top shelf wasn't in the cards for me that day. Then again, based on what I'd seen of the clientele of this place, those expensive bottles would probably be covered in dust.

When the bartender brought me my glass, I slipped the card Jimmy had given me across the bar.

Instead of picking it up, the bartender reached under the bar for a long metal tube, about three inches wide and a foot long. It made a weird humming noise when he turned it on, and emitted a creepy purple glow.

The card turned bright white under the light. Words that I couldn't see before suddenly showed up. The top of the card had "Jimmy" printed on it. Underneath the GE, which now appeared a bright green color, was the single word, "Double."

I was impressed by the security. I might have to get me one of those glow lights, except that I wasn't planning on working a lot of drug cases. Even drugs that weren't supposed to do anyone harm.

The bartender took the card, then reached under the bar again for a box. It was four inches a side, and about that tall as well. Inside, nestled in what looked like blue satin, sat two well-cushioned eggs. They were each about the size of a small chicken egg. But that was where the similarities ended.

I could tell the difference immediately between the two eggs. The Golden Egg was, well, golden. Thin lines of black crisscrossed the surface, like a miniature stained-glass window. The gold wasn't even. It faded to yellow in some areas, and grew really rich and dark in others, like amber holding the black bodies of insects. I didn't pick the delicate Golden Egg up, but I did touch it, and was surprised by how warm the surface felt.

The Dragon Egg was a bright green color, the same hue as the letters on the card had been when looked at under the special light. The lines on the egg were thicker, and the color was more consistent. It, too, was very warm.

For a brief moment, I thought I smelled Carol's rainlike perfume.

The bartender quoted me a price for the pair of them.

I debated. Mrs. Wagner was certainly paying me enough to justify getting them. But I would never use them myself, either of them. That way lay sure madness and hell.

I bargained the bartender down slightly before I paid, determined to claim this purchase as an expense and to charge Mrs. Wagner for it. I'd have to figure out how to write up an invoice for them later.

I mean, buying these was purely case-related, right?

THE BOX WAS TOO BULKY TO FIT IN A JACKET POCKET. However, I couldn't ditch it and take a chance on putting the eggs unprotected into a pocket—they'd be sure to break. I didn't have a briefcase or something handy to hide the box in either. Instead, I walked to the nearest green grocer and bought a couple of cans of ham and beans, the kind I could easily heat up on the hotplate in my room for lunch. I slipped the box into the paper bag and caught the train back to my office.

Trains traveled in their own tunnels, away from the good people of the city who used expensive private taxies. The train was like the staff entrance of any hotel—very busy and fully occupied by working stiffs. There wasn't anything to see out the windows, just tunnels carved through the rock with the occasional control box. Hell, even the platforms weren't anything to look at, just a name and an opening.

The box that I held in my lap felt as though it were burning a hole through the paper bag.

I'd never been tempted by a drug before. What had happened to Mom had scared me but good. Whiskey was about as hard as I ever did. And while I probably drank more than the average Joe, I wasn't worried about it. There were too many times when I had to cut myself off, go dry when the clients had run out and I didn't have the cash even for rotgut.

Since I could always stop and start the drink, I figured it didn't have its claws too far into me.

This though—this was the unknown temptress. What would it be like to lose that all-too-familiar sense of melancholy that stuck with me like the constant dryness in the air? To feel happy, truly happy, just for a while? Was it worth getting out from under the yoke of depression? Or would I end up just as miserable on the other side of this trip?

I truly didn't know. And honestly, I was too much of a coward to find out.

My office looked the same at it always did, a little dingy and down on its luck, but the corners were clean and the rest of the room tidy. The sweet smell of Carol's perfume still lingered, that rainy scent that made me think of lush green jungles.

Someday, if I could ever afford it, I planned on visiting Earth and traveling to someplace really rainy, like Seattle, just to sit in the middle of a park during a downpour. I couldn't imagine it, not really, rain just hammering down from the sky that way. I'd never made enough credits to take a wet shower. I took dry ones, with refreshers wicking away the sweat and constant dust.

I sat with the box on my desk, the lights low, contemplating the two eggs. Turned out that in the dim light, they had their own slight glow.

According to everything I knew, Golden Eggs were relatively harmless. Crush the shell, get one quick puff of euphoria, and it was gone.

Then why had Central banned them? Was there something else going on? And not just officials being bribed to keep them off the market?

And what the heck would a Dragon Egg do? My gut told me that the two started off with the same base material, that egg. But some scientist along the way had tweaked it, given the green egg an advantage.

They were both tempting.

Too tempting.

Instead of even picking either of them up, I closed up their travel box and locked it away in one of my filing cabinets. Trials for another day.

In the meanwhile, I had just enough time to get back to my boarding house, snag some dinner, then change into my better second-hand suit, polish my shoes, and go out to see where *fondue* might lead me.

THE PIEDMONT LOOKED THE SAME AS IT HAD, THOUGH with fewer bellhops. The crowd in the lobby looked a bit more dressed to kill, or maybe, dressed after having killed, based on the number of fur stoles I saw on the dames, and more than one gent with a fur collar or cuffs on his overcoat.

I didn't know why people bothered. Central always kept the corridors at the same temperature. No one ever needed a jacket or sweater.

That extra clothing was probably just one more way the top cats broadcast their rank to us plebeians. I hadn't dressed up—if I was already staying at the hotel, I wouldn't be forced to overdress that way. Or at least that was my reckoning.

A different hatchet lady worked as the elevator attendant —the other one's sister, perhaps. They shared the same hawk-like nose and bad temper, though this one's gray hair had a touch of blue added to it.

At least four other people got into the cage with me. I slipped the attendant a small bill, as some of the others had when they'd entered, then asked in a quiet voice, "My wife's in the mood for some fondue. Would you be able to recommend a place?"

"Maybe," the woman growled, her voice surprisingly deep and gravely. "I'll have to think about it."

She dropped off the other guests before turning to me with a glittering smile. "I know just the place for you," she said.

The way she was eying me like fresh bait made me a bit nervous. "I'm game," I told her blandly.

"One fondue, coming right up," she said.

As I'd suspected, the handle used to guide the elevator turned out to be a fantastic way to hide floors. Plus, since no one could count the stories from the outside, that extra space was easy to hide.

"Fondue," she said with a cackle as she opened the door somewhere between floors three and four.

"Thank you," I said, sliding her another bill before I stepped into the room.

The first thing that struck me was that strong perfume again, that I'd smelled earlier downstairs. I'd assumed it was from the performers, and I may have been right. But it was sweeter now, almost sickly sweet.

It reminded me of something, though I couldn't put my finger on it.

The edges of the room were dim enough to conduct private business, partners able to slip through the shadows without being seen or recognized, while the center of the room was lit up like Central had decided to throw a party. A tall stage was set up at the end of it, with a live band to one side. Whatever show was going to play that night hadn't started yet.

Thick red carpet covered the floor. Despite how merry the three dozen attendees appeared to be, the noise wasn't overwhelming. Maybe that was in part because the ceiling was almost eighteen feet high—an uncomfortably tall space for a warren rat like me.

It was difficult to make out exactly where the walls of the room lay. Still, I had the impression that the space was pretty large, maybe thirty foot on a side. There was no bar where a fella could go order himself a drink, no, you were required to be civilized here and only order through the circulating waiters. They all wore white suit jackets, decorated with navy blue braid around the cuffs and down the front.

I made my way to a small table on the side of the main stage. It had a heavy linen tablecloth, a crystal vase with a single rose in it, and a menu listing prices that were suited to maintain this joint.

Yet another business expense with no receipt.

The lights didn't dim as the sole dancer came out. A sultry Human woman, tall with raven black hair, pale skin, and ruby red lips. Her eyes had a far-away look, as if a mountain in the distance had caught her attention and was sending her cool air on its breezes.

She looked like a torch singer, wearing a crimson satin outfit, with matching long gloves and a white fur stole. The band struck up a quietly seductive number, much smoother and jazzier than what they'd been playing.

When the first glove came off, the rest of the room grew quieter, watching.

She was mesmerizing as she slunk across the floor, removing a shoe, turning her back to remove a single stocking, teasing the audience with backwards glances and that nervous biting of her lip.

Though the dancer was Human, that hesitation reminded me strongly of Carol.

It was an artistic strip show, I had to give them that. Very athletic, with twists and turns that only a true acrobat would generally be capable of, bending backward and almost touching the floor at one point.

Gave a man ideas when a woman was that flexible.

When the final bits came off, I realized why this was an illegal show, despite the demure, artistic approach to stripping. Everything had been bared to the audience. I wondered if rouge had been applied to her nipples as they were the same ruby red color as her lips. And the carpet matched the drapes, both that raven black color.

It made me uncomfortable being able to see so much, but the other men in the club applauded and cheered. Seemed as though that was normal, here.

The next act was similar, though instead of dressed up like a torch singer the burlesque dancer started off dressed in a French maid's uniform, complete with feather duster.

The third show finally explained the password. She wore a plain sheath dress and pushed what looked like a dessert cart with her onto the stage. As part of her act, she dripped both chocolate and strawberry sauce over her body, sprinkling her skin with peanuts and candy, before using whipped cream to "top" everything off.

I guess she was going for "good enough to eat." Turned my stomach, frankly. Though I appreciated the artistry, it was all too out in the open for me. I preferred to be teased more, rather than having it all be so blatant.

What was very interesting, however, was that I saw a waiter present a small box to one of the nearby tables. The box looked identical to what I'd bought that afternoon. Plus, the mild glow that shone when the gentleman opened his box made me assume it was the same.

The way to take a Golden Egg was to crush it completely, then inhale all the fumes released from it.

A new wave of that sickly sweet perfume washed over me when the gentleman did just that.

Earlier, I hadn't been smelling the perfume of the guests or the girls.

It was from the drugs themselves.

WHAT DID IT MEAN THAT THERE WERE ENOUGH DRUGS being used in the hotel that they'd stink up the lobby? That they were being "served" to guests, instead of having to be bought in some back alley or dive bar? What had I gotten myself into?

I had to remind myself that I wasn't investigating the drug trade, no, just the disappearance of one of the major suppliers.

The next morning, after a sleepless night filled with nightmares of Mom, who had black holes for eyes urging me to just try one, it would be fine, I made it to my office just in time to meet the courier in the hallway. He carried with him a brown leather valise, well worn, maybe two feet long and a foot tall.

I signed for it, tipping the man just a few coins, before carrying it back into my office.

Damned place still carried a hint of Carol Wagner's perfume, that wet smell. But now it was tinged with a sweetness that I recognized from the Golden Eggs.

I turned the overhead fan on high to try to get rid of the smell before I checked the eggs themselves.

The eggs actually didn't have a scent when I opened the box. Strange. Was that sweetness just in my imagination? No, I still smelled it.

I locked the eggs back up tightly, momentarily wishing that I'd actually bought a safe that would take more than just determination to break into.

Maybe once this case was over, given Mrs. Wagner's initial generosity…

I put the bag on the middle of my desk, then turned a light on it directly. I slid my hands around the outside of it, sliding my fingers across the smooth leather, giving myself a solid feel for the actual dimensions of the bag. Just because I was paranoid, I gave the bag a good sniff before I opened it, but all I could smell was leather and a man's subtle cologne, something spicy like Bay Rum.

No pockets marred the lines on the outside of the bag. Unsurprisingly, when I unzipped it, I found lots of pockets on the inside.

Neatly folded shirts and underwear filled most of the center compartment. I could tell they'd all been worn recently, as well as the socks stuck at the bottom. No pants or suit jacket—he probably hadn't felt the need to change. His bathroom kit contained a depilatory cream, the kind used to get rid of that five o'clock shadow and make your chin silky smooth for a night out on the town. Or so the commercials promised.

That surprised me. Wouldn't an important man like Mr. Wagner go to a nearby barber to have his daily shave? It certainly was something he could afford. Hell, I would figure that he'd go to one of those fancy places that used real water and hot towels.

After I removed everything from the bag, I started searching for hidden compartments. I compared the outside of the bag to the bottom of the inside of the bag, not finding anything obvious. I patted the inside as well as the outside along both sides, trying to find a hidden pocket.

Nothing.

Surely Mr. Wagner wasn't that smart, was he? To carry nothing with him of what I was sure was his "other" business here on the moon?

The zippered opening wasn't wide enough to let me turn the bag inside out, and Mrs. Wagner wouldn't be pleased if I broke the valise. I held the bag up between my two hands, one inside the bag with my fingers spread across the bottom, the other on the outside.

Bingo. A slight discrepancy.

I managed to pry up one of the corners of the bottom of the bag. My fingers identified what there were before I drew them out.

Glossies.

There were black and white photos of the last girl at the show the night before, the one who poured sauce on herself.

Fondue.

The first two pictures were obvious professional stills, taken of the girl while she performed her routine, first half naked, and the second, artistically covered with sauce and candy bits, holding the whipped cream canister up high in one hand, as if about to shoot it all over her face.

The last two were done by an amateur. The first showed the girl smiling coyly at the camera, face on, with one arm demurely covering her bare breasts. The second showed her from behind, on her hands and knees, completely nude, looking over her shoulder and winking at the camera.

These pictures didn't have the whiff of chemicals that I associated with developed film.

No, they smelled of the sweet drug Mr. Wagner peddled.

So, he was having an affair while he was here. A well-hidden affair, as I doubted that Mrs. Wagner would let him loose on his own.

I shuddered at the thought of what she could do with

those teeth to a Human male's, uhm, *bits*, if she ever got really angry.

Was the girl the key to Mr. Wagner's disappearance? Had he decided that it was better to date a Human burlesque dancer rather than stay with an alien? Or was there something else going on? And did Jimmy the Skunk have anything to do with it?

I had too many questions, and the gut feeling that I was running out of time. Mr. Wagner had been missing for half a month at that point, fifteen days. Was he even still alive? Or had he found a better place to be?

I put all the clothing carefully back into the case, just as I'd found it, while I locked the pictures with my notes back into my filing cabinet.

Time to go put the squeeze on old Jimmy, see if he could fill me in on the movements of his supplier.

IT TOOK ME SOME TIME TO GET A BEAD ON WHERE Jimmy was staying when he wasn't working. Seemed the dispute with his former boss had been pretty severe, and Jimmy had taken to never spending more than three nights in any one place. He moved from staying with friends to a cheap hotel, then back to friends.

Fortunately, I ran into a guy who owed me a favor, on account of tracking down not only his ex, but where she'd hidden all his stuff. He was in a similar business to Jimmy, though he tended to play cards at joints a step up from a dive like the Gin Mill.

I walked up to the apartment building just in time to see Jimmy walking out. I figured he was heading to the Gin Mill, so I only tailed him for a block or so, making sure I'd guessed right, before I stretched my legs and caught up with him. He was wearing the same suit as the day before, and he hadn't found a barber yet to dye his hair.

"Hey, Jimmy," I called out, all friendly like.

He startled bad, as if he'd just been caught with his hand in the till. He didn't relax until he saw who it was.

"Hey, Alvin," he said, giving me a crooked grin. "Did I steer you right or what?"

"You sure did," I told him, grinning. "But, ah, now I got a friend. You know? Who might be looking for something like what I bought."

"I got you covered," Jimmy said. The look he gave me was smug satisfaction, not surprise.

Seemed as though he'd expected me finding him today, to ask about purchasing more of the drug.

Good to know.

I looked over my shoulder, as if checking to make sure no one was following us. "I, uh, got the cash. Can I give it to you now, and come and pick up my shipment later?"

"Sure thing!" Jimmy said, all friendly and accommodating.

We stepped into an alley just off the street.

Fortunately, Jimmy wasn't expecting a thing, so once we were hidden from casual view, I threw him hard up against the wall, then kept him there with one hand on his shoulder, my forearm across his neck, choking off any foolish cries for help that he might have given.

"Listen, you pipsqueak," I growled. "I don't care what you're selling or to whom. What I care about is your supplier. Richard Wagner. Heard of him?"

Jimmy gave a choked laugh. "I'd wondered which dimwit was going to take that case."

That gave me pause. I loosened my hold slightly so Jimmy was getting a bit more air. Not enough for him to twist out of it, though. "You know he's missing?"

"Course I do. Everyone does," Jimmy said, trying for a glare but his eyes were still too wide and he still looked too scared around the edges.

"What's the over-under?" I asked.

"Either that he offed himself rather than return to that harridan of a wife, or he's run off with some bimbo," Jimmy replied. "Probably off world."

The pictures in the bottom of his suitcase led me to believe that he hadn't run off with his mistress, at least not the one I'd seen last night at the show. That left the first option—which meant that the honorable Mr. Wagner was lying dead in a tunnel somewhere and the cops either hadn't found the body, or they hadn't identified it yet.

"Thanks," I said, releasing Jimmy and stepping back.

Instead of scurrying away as I'd expected, Jimmy stayed where he was, peering at me in the dim alley. "You didn't take either the Golden Egg or the Dragon Egg, did you?"

I shook my head, though I wasn't about to explain my own personal history with my mom's addiction.

"Didn't think so. The eggs always leave a guy feeling happy, at least for a while. Too happy to come and rough someone up in an alley."

I gave a nonchalant shrug. That was just how business was done. Jimmy understood that.

"Yeah, happy, mostly, until the eggs aren't enough anymore. Like if a guy's got such a shit hand in life that nothing will work," Jimmy added pointedly. "Not even the Dragon Eggs."

"Why are you telling me this?" I asked, assuming that there was a connection between what Jimmy was saying and my missing mogul.

Jimmy shrugged. "I always felt sorry for the guy, you know? Wagner. His wife kept him on a really short leash.

He'd sometimes have to leave a meeting in the middle of it just to call her."

"Yeah, I know," I said, though I hadn't at all. I took a quick breath, holding in my temper until later. "She really wants him back."

"Good luck," Jimmy said. "I'd try the morgue first for this one." Then he sauntered off, as if he'd been the one who'd suggested meeting in this alley in the first place.

I stayed where I was, my anger washing over me.

Once again, I'd believed the dame with the sob story. I should have known better.

I *did* know better. What had gotten me to overlook one of the first rules of investigating? When something felt fishy, always check the client first. Their hands were rarely clean.

That sweet, wet smell of her perfume came back to me. How similar it was to the smell of the drugs.

There was some connection there, something I just wasn't seeing.

But what?

My phone was ringing when I walked into the office. Given what I'd just learned of Mrs. Wagner, it didn't surprise me. Was probably her on the other end, demanding an update.

I wasn't rich enough to have something like an answering service. Sure, I probably could have afforded it. But that would have meant actually being willing to take calls day or night. I wasn't about to offer that level of service.

I ignored the call, letting the phone ring until the other party hung up.

Then I sat down with my feet up on my desk, thinking through what I'd learned that afternoon. I'd stopped by the morgue on my way in, handing the cops the picture of Richard that Carol had given me earlier.

Sure enough, they had a John Doe on ice who matched the photo and description. They were surprised that the wife hadn't called him in as missing, as they'd had him for a few days. They'd found the body hanging down in one of the tunnels, near Blind-Man's Alley, a place famous, or even infamous, for foul play.

However, they hadn't been able to find anything on the body that indicated something other than a suicide. No bruising to indicate a recent fight, no scratch marks. No note, either, just the body hanging from a pipe, a kicked over chair underneath.

He'd been hanging there for a while, that much they knew, as it had been the smell that had finally drawn someone to the body to report it.

That sickly, sweet smell of drugs and rotting flesh.

The cops figured that he might have left a note in his wallet, but whoever had first found the body had stripped the wallet as well as the watch and rings from it. Even his shoes and jacket had been stolen.

I didn't like thinking about the kind of desperation it took to strip a dead body. I'd been around a few corpses in my line of work. Not anything that I would ever grow used to.

I promised myself that I'd quit before I grew that blasé.

I didn't have to wait long before Mrs. Wagner came slinking back into my office. It really did amaze me at how sexy she walked. As if she'd studied it, become a master of it.

Possibly from someone who made the art of movement seduction itself. Like a former burlesque dancer before she'd found "love."

She wore another sheath dress that day, this one somber

blue, though with the same white stole and hair. She looked like a vision of wealth itself.

"The police came to visit me this afternoon," Mrs. Wagner said before she sank back down in one of the guest chairs. She seemed oddly defeated, resigned to the world and all the awfulness that was sure to rain down on her.

"I'm sorry for your loss," I told her sincerely. Didn't matter what sort of relationship they'd had. It was still a loss that would make some parts of the world a little more empty and cold.

She gave a bitter laugh. "So am I. Now I'm going to need to find a new partner for my eggs."

"Your eggs?" I asked, surprised. "Were the Golden Eggs found on your property? I thought that the eggs were mined under the jungles on Venus."

"You silly Human," she chided. "You know, you shouldn't believe everything you're told."

I knew that. I'd already had my nose rubbed in it once that day.

"So where do the eggs come from?" I asked. I was pretty sure I wasn't going to like the answer, but I figured it was better to know.

"From me," she said.

"What?"

"You Humans have understood very little of the Venusian birth cycle," she said. "Though we've told your scientists again and again. They still seem to think it's quaint and keep tinkering, as if it's something that needs to be fixed."

"Okay," I said, not following at all.

"Like Human offspring, ours start as eggs," Carol said primly, like a schoolmarm lecturing an unwilling student. "Unlike Human women, we have the option of either carrying the eggs inside our body, or outside of it."

"I see," I said. I didn't like where this was going, though. Not at all. But I wasn't about to reach for the ray gun sitting next to the whiskey bottle in the bottom drawer. This didn't strike me as a do-or-die moment for Carol.

Not yet.

"With the right Human mate, those sacs of eggs can turn into gold," Carol said. She gave me a dreamy look. "All that gold, just for the taking."

How many mates had Carol gone through before she'd found Richard Wagner, the Human male who could help her manufacture Golden Eggs? What had she been doing to entice them to her lair?

"I don't want to know any more details," I told her, holding up my hand. It turned my stomach.

"Oh, don't worry," Carol said. "There are plenty of egg breeders who just produce offspring. There's no concern about the race suddenly dying out, having sold too many of our potential children."

I couldn't help but shudder at her matter-of-fact tone.

"You sure you don't want to try out? Audition for the part?" Carol teased, her voice growing low and seductive. "I've been trained by the best in the business. You'd be well satisfied. And rich beyond your wildest dreams if you turned out to be the right partner."

"Not with those teeth, lady," I said, bluntly honest.

That got me what could have been a real laugh. Or maybe not. I wouldn't ever know what was real and what wasn't with this alien.

"I like you," Carol said as she stood, adjusting her dress and jiggling in what was always going to be a disturbing manner. "I'll call on you the next time I come to the moon."

With that, she swept out of my office, leaving just her sweet perfume behind.

What an idiot I'd been. What had let me to believing a

dame and not taking the time to investigate the client first? Had it been her sweet smell and sweeter body that had gotten me, a man who knew better, to overlook the basics?

Temptation and greed. Fortunately not a lethal combination…this time.

After she'd gone, I locked the door to my office, not wanting to be disturbed. Then I finally checked the lock on the file cabinet where I kept the notes for this case.

Yup. Someone had jiggered it open recently. Probably Carol Wagner, looking over my notes to see if there was something I wasn't telling her. No wonder that scent of her perfume had lingered.

I realized that I'd never given her a bill for all those extra expenses I'd incurred. I wasn't sure I wanted to even invoice her. She might pay. Or she might not, and instead, come back to persuade me to do a barter for "services rendered."

There was no way of knowing beforehand if I would turn out to be the right Human mate for the job of fertilizing her eggs, getting them to turn to gold.

I shuddered again, going back to my desk and taking a sharp hit of whiskey before I pulled out the box with the Golden Egg and Dragon Egg nestled inside.

I took the top off the box, put it on the center of my desk blotter, put my feet back up on the desk and contemplated what I'd learned.

Knowing that the eggs had a biological start wouldn't give any junky pause. But it might be why Central continued to ban the things. Didn't know what process would turn the Golden Eggs into Dragon Eggs, which was yet another reason for Central to ban them. Particularly if the latter were addictive, and I would bet they were given how Jimmy the Skunk had appeared to be expecting me.

But the monkey had already climbed out of the barrel on this one. Didn't think they'd ever be able to put it back.

So I sat in my office with the lights dim, this time slowly sipping two fingers of whiskey, the eggs shining with their own light, that faintly sweet smell drawing me closer, making me reach out and gently rub one finger against the warm shell, only to sit back again and think, time and again.

I had enough vices in my life. I didn't need one more.

And yet...

[2]

THE CASE OF THE VANISHING CREAM

THERE WASN'T MUCH I COULD DO FOR MRS. KELMER. Sure, her baby girl Jenny had gone missing. Sure, it was a cold hard place out here on the moon, particularly in the tunnels underneath the cities. Sure, maybe there had been foul play.

But only maybe. There was no evidence of that, not really.

It was that last point that kept me from diving headlong into some sort of idiotic knight-in-shining-armor routine.

With a name like Alvin Goodfellow, I got a lot of hard-luck cases, shmucks who thought they could sucker me into working for free. As the jingle proclaimed, as well as the ads I paid good money for, I was the PI to the stars, the best you could hire on the moon, Venus, or Mars, (though I only had this one office on the moon).

But my time came at a price, and I was upfront with Mrs. Kelmer about exactly what my fees were going to be. Particularly when Jenny Kelmer turned out to be a twenty-something young woman who'd had a fight with her mother just before she'd stormed off, not a twelve-year-old girl missing from school.

The police wouldn't touch the case. Particularly not after Mrs. Kelmer told them that Jenny had been planning this break for a while. She currently lived at the dorm, but had intended to not move back home once the semester was finished. She'd already rented an apartment on the far side of the city.

I agreed with Mrs. Kelmer that it was suspicious that Jenny had never actually arrived back at the dorm. However, if Mrs. Kelmer had been my mother, I probably would have left a false trail or two too, just to get away from her.

Mrs. Kelmer favored me with a disgruntled *hrumph* once she heard how much I was going to charge her. "Are you sure you couldn't waive your fees? Just this once?"

I'd taken on more than one charity case over the course of my career. They almost always turned around and bit me in the ass before I'd finished them.

More to the point, Mrs. Kelmer didn't look like someone who relied on the kindness of strangers.

Central kept the air a steady seventy degrees, no matter where you went. You didn't need rain jackets, hats, or gloves.

Mrs. Kelmer wore all three, which spoke of money, and the need to maintain certain standards. Only the rich showed up in extra, unnecessary clothing. Her auburn hair had a perfect curl in the back, and she had to be regularly going to an expensive hairdresser to maintain that in the dryness of the air here. Her skin was a fashionable shade of white, with sculpted eyebrows and red lips that pouted beautifully, which probably worked on your average, garden variety mook.

Not me.

"I'm not sure why I would need to waive my fees," I told her, gesturing toward her so that she could possibly take a look at herself. Not that I expected someone like her to have the least bit of self-awareness. No, it usually had to be pointed out to them explicitly. "Look around you. Do I appear to be a man of means?"

The office wasn't a complete dive, no matter what my mother might have said had she ever gotten out of the clinic and come to visit. It was located in the Stockton Warrens in the main city of the moon, with the stupid fishbowl windows protruding out to the outer corridor just behind my desk. I kept the shades drawn tightly across them, as who wanted to see poor factory workers stumbling along when the shift changed?

Three dinged-up, secondhand file cabinets sat in one corner, filled with notes from previous cases. Locked of course, though anyone who came equipped with a good quality paperclip could break into them. A water cooler burbled to itself in the other corner, a sound I found comforting. One of my clients told me that it reminded him of the splashing of a fountain, a sound I'd never heard first-hand. I didn't know if even the ultrarich could afford such a luxury on the moon, all that water running freely.

My desk was large and though it looked like wood, it wasn't, of course. Just good, sturdy metal. It worked as an effective enough breaker for the poor slobs who expected me to come leaping to their defense or aid. Comfortable chair on my side. Less comfortable chairs on the other side. Lazy fan in the center of the ceiling, more for show than for actually moving around the stale air that Central piped in.

Mrs. Kelmer made a show of looking around my office. Probably measuring the amount of dust in the corners. "You know what I see? A man who has made it."

At my derisive snort, she held up a gloved hand. "Hear me out. You report to no one but yourself. Set your own hours. Take what cases you please. Drink a little too much some afternoons," she added with a disapproving sniff, "but you're no drunk."

I shrugged. She'd actually gotten most of that right. I couldn't always take just the easy cases. I had too many damned expenses to turn down all the nasty clients. The ones that I was sure would give me trouble just got a PITAT added to them—a pain in the ass tax. I'd never been a model employee. Asked too many annoying questions as opposed to just doing as I'd been told, and couldn't stand a nine-to-five routine.

"You might see me and think, *money*," Mrs. Kelmer continued. "That's not completely accurate, though. My husband controls all of it. I get a pitiable allowance. And I have to turn in all my receipts to him. Then I get raked over the coals if there are any discrepancies." She rolled her eyes at that. "It's all such nonsense! I am a grown woman. I should be able to control my own finances."

I didn't ask her why she didn't. In my experience, if a husband was that controlling, there was generally a reason for it.

Instead, I asked, "And you really want to bring your daughter back into that household?"

My words may have sounded a bit cruel, but I needed her to catch a clue. If that was possible.

Mrs. Kelmer bit her bright red lip with her perfectly white teeth, perfectly aligned. She just didn't get it, didn't understand how far apart we actually were. How I'd been brought up on the wrong side of the spaceport, as it were. My teeth were only straight due to good genes, not because I could afford the right dentistry. I still had a baby face, with red hair that I kept shorn close to my head because otherwise it curled outrageously, even someplace as dry as the moon.

"I see your point, I really do," Mrs. Kelmer sighed after a bit. "But Jenny—she wouldn't just disappear that way! She would have left a message to let me know that she was all right. Something."

"Maybe you can save up some of that allowance money and come see me in a couple of weeks if you still haven't heard from your daughter," I said. Then I added, "I don't work for free."

Mrs. Kelmer stood up. "No, you work for money. I had hoped that you had a heart as well, and could understand a mother's pain."

Bringing up motherhood was never a good idea with me. I still stood up and told her, "Look. I will not take your case. Not without something upfront. But I will keep my ears open. If I hear anything about a Jenny or any other missing girls, I'll let you know."

"Fine," Mrs. Kelmer said. She swept out of the room.

Her dramatic exit was spoiled though, as she wasn't able to slam the door behind her with a resounding clang. A man was coming in just as she was leaving.

I didn't know this individual either. Fortunately, I was already standing. "Good afternoon," I said. Hopefully this would be a client who was actually prepared to pay.

He looked like an insurance salesman. You know the type. Nervous, bobbing, balding head. Compulsive swallower. Not a stammer, but a collection of other nervous ticks. Dressed in a shirt and tie, nice slacks, no jacket. Not a factory worker, but an office employee.

The kind who were either richer than Croesus and hid it well, or who were loonier than the poor mutants who lived in the tunnels under the city.

Hopefully not both.

"Mr. Goodfellow?" the man asked, staying next to the door.

"Yes?" I said. I also stayed where I was behind my nice, safe desk.

"My property's been stolen from me. I'd like for you to find it and return it."

Finally, a reasonable, straight-forward case!

"Certainly. Please, have a seat. Tell me about it," I said, sitting back down.

The man gulped and nodded, as I knew he would.

"I'd rather show you, if that's all right?" When he saw my hesitation, he added, "I'm happy to pay you for your time." He pulled a wad of bills from his pocket. "Just…I need you to come and see."

I had a bad feeling about his insistence that I come and see the scene of the crime. Still, I had already turned down one case that afternoon. The second one had to be better, right?

MR. DINKLEWOOD—OR LARRY, AS HE INSISTED THAT I call him—did, in fact, work as an insurance broker. He spent our time walking to and from the train stations trying to convince me that it wasn't a scam, that someone who worked as their own boss must have some sort of coverage in case they had an accident or if they needed to take an extended leave of absence.

All insurance was a con, and I knew it. I tried to put Larry off as best I could, telling him that I had my own sort of insurance (a meager savings account) as well as investments (a year's rent already paid ahead on my tiny apartment, courtesy of one of my last big cases).

The trains ran in their own separate tunnels, out of sight of people like Mrs. Kelmer who probably took very expensive private taxies wherever they needed to go. It was midafternoon, so between shift breaks. Not many people were in the cars at that point, just a group of obnoxious teenaged tourists from Earth who probably thought of this as a wild adventure, getting so far off the beaten path and away from the clean, shiny parts of the city.

I resented being someone else's cultural experience. I was just a regular Joe who lived and worked there, on the Moon.

Larry and I exited on the eastern side of the city, near the warehouse district. It wasn't a bad neighborhood, but it was hardly a residential area. Huge hulking buildings filled either side of the mostly empty street. Property would be shipped via dedicated supply trains from the spaceport to the center of the district, then carted away to its final destination with huge forklifts and specialized trucks.

Once at the proper warehouse, additional manufacturing or assembly could be done before the goods would be ready for consumption.

I had thought that Larry would be taking me back to his apartment. "Where was your property located?" I finally thought to ask as he hurried along, making me nearly run to keep up. Up ahead, one of the large forklifts trundled along, its load lifted high above the cabin where the driver sat. The air was more stale here, probably because not many people were moving and adding to the air circulation.

"This way," Larry said in response. He led the way to a self-storage unit that was tucked away between two huge warehouses.

Huh. Owning a storage unit generally meant that someone had a whole lot of cash, as well as a heck of a lot of things that needed storing.

Maybe taking good ol' Larry on as a client wasn't such a bad choice. Or at least that was what I told myself, trying to soothe the unease I had in my gut.

Larry pulled out his keys, then looked over both his shoulders to make sure that no one was around. Other than me.

The lock came undone with a heavy *thunk*. I would bet that it hadn't been the original lock on the door, that Larry had replaced it after his property had been stolen. Would take a lot more than just a paperclip and a lot of enthusiasm to pick that lock.

He rolled up the large garage door just a few feet. Lights suddenly shone out from the opening.

"Quickly!" Larry said, motioning me forward.

Fine. I wasn't looking forward to walking into a new place bent in half. Seemed I had no choice, though.

I ducked under the door, ready for anything.

Except a mad scientist's lab.

LARRY JOINED ME PROMPTLY ON THE OTHER SIDE OF the garage door. I figured that whatever he was doing here was completely illegal. Hopefully Central never got wind of it. No wonder he'd come to me and not the cops.

Still, as he was paying me for my time (and I was keeping close track of it, rounding up in fifteen-minute increments) I was going to at least listen to what the man had to say.

Bright white lights shone down from the ceiling, illuminating everything harshly. I was surprised that Larry's balding head hadn't gotten a sunburn from being under them. Workbenches stretched along all three walls. Test tubes, Bunsen burners, and vials of glowing chemicals were precisely placed on each. It smelled like burnt lemons in here, a sickly sweet, yet charred smell. The air was cooler in here than the usual ambient temperature of the moon warrens. I could hear the fans blowing from the corners. Maybe to keep the scent of his experiments from accumulating? So that no one would know he was here?

An old-fashioned still was running off to the side, the

copper kettle bubbling along. The process appeared to be distilling a blue gas that was being syphoned off the top, up along the curling plastic pipe, then dripped into a large black vat.

"So what exactly was stolen?" I asked, looking around. I didn't see any broken glass or any obvious holes in the masses of equipment.

"My latest experiment," Larry said woefully.

"Which was?" I prompted when Larry just stood there, wringing his hands.

"It wasn't the fountain of youth, though I imagine, when I finally make an announcement to the papers, that will be precisely the headline that some smart-alecky reporter will come up with," Larry said, his tone sliding between pride and disparagement.

"So what was it?"

"This is what I wanted to show you," Larry said. He hurried over to the side, to the large refrigeration unit humming to itself. He pulled out a flat board, maybe two feet on a side. It had three-inch-square samples hanging in precise rows, each labeled and dated in neat black letters.

"I wanted to show you the results of what I'd been working with, so that you would understand the importance of my work," Larry continued. "I didn't want you to just take my word that what I've made is world changing."

I made a gesture to get Larry to continue with his explanation and to stop grandstanding.

"Look here," Larry said, starting up at the top left corner. "Now, compare that sample to this one," he said, pointing to the end of the line. "You see how much younger the skin has grown? How the aging process at first diminishes, then reverses?"

It took me a few moments to realize that I was looking at samples of skin.

Human skin.

"Where exactly did you get your samples?" I said. I didn't take a step back but I did take a deeper breath to see if that too-familiar stench of decomp lingered in the air.

Who knew what else Larry was storing in that refrigeration unit of his?

"Oh, don't worry," Larry told me hurriedly. "I have a friend who works at the city morgue."

So in addition to running an illegal lab, good ol' Larry was a graverobber.

Swell.

I looked at the various samples, listening to Larry's explanation of application times and amounts, before I had to ask, "This sure looks impressive. But does it only work on dead skin?"

I mean, there wasn't much market for making a corpse prettier, was there? (Was there?) Particularly since Central had a strict policy of cremation if the body stayed here, on the Moon. Wasn't any of their business what happened once the body got shipped off planet.

Knew more than one enterprising soul who was making a good living sending bodies spinning up in orbit. Wasn't where I wanted to go. Rather be cremated, as I was sure to be burning in Hell by that point already.

"No, no, it works just as well on living flesh! I can show you the pictures, but they aren't as impressive as the samples," Larry said, looking fondly at his board. His hand hesitated, rising up toward it, as if he were about to stroke the flesh there.

Yuck.

"So what exactly happened?" I said, now that I was willing to believe that Larry had, indeed, invented something worth stealing. Lots of women would want younger-looking skin.

"I was working with several different females," Larry said. "Human as well as alien. It was all under the table sort of work. Cost me a pretty penny, too, getting the girls to come here. But it was worth it," he assured me. "All those payments were just investments in my future."

I was sure he had an amortization table already worked out, showing just how those future payments would go.

I gestured for Larry to go on. His nervous habit of pausing between sentences was going to drive me crazy sooner rather than later.

Larry led me to the right, behind the still.

Finally, I saw the evidence of what he'd been talking about. I had no idea what was missing. However, even I could see the void there, where several bottles had at one time stood.

"Someone broke in and stole some of the completed product?" I said as Larry continued to stand there, head bowed in mourning.

"All of it, all that I had finished making. As well as my notes," Larry said, pulling open a drawer that was completely empty. He looked absolutely wracked, as though someone had stolen his child.

He certainly seemed more upset than Mrs. Kelmer had, earlier in my office, which had been yet another reason why I hadn't taken her case. Something had just seemed off about the entire affair.

"What does that mean?" I said, wanting him to spell out all the details. "That they've taken your notes?"

"I can't recreate everything!" Larry whined.

"Really?" I said. Was he serious about that? "Don't you have a backup set of notes somewhere?"

"No!" Larry said. "I couldn't trust that something wouldn't happen to them. I know what the actuary tables say. I knew that out here, my chances of being robbed were negligible, at least compared to the rates of crime that happen in my neighborhood, on my block."

That made sense to me. Larry had been making a lot of money as an insurance salesman, probably not only getting a percentage of every sale, but skimming off the payments that people made into the system, as well as a good cut of everything that his company paid out.

If they paid out at all. Chances were that some of the payoffs never made it to the actual customers, but went to outfitting Larry with better equipment for his lab.

However, a mook like Larry wouldn't spend any of that money on himself. He probably lived in a dreary little flat, one room, a pullout Murphy bed on the wall. He'd eat his meals over the sink, no table to sit at, no chairs or living room to entertain friends in. I'd bet he had a party line coming into the building as well.

Yup. Larry probably lived like a monk, in poverty and filth, only getting cleaned up to come to the lab.

"So you really can't recreate everything?" I said. I had to clarify that point. It made no sense to me. Then again, I wasn't an expert when it came to scientific experimentation. Particularly mad science, like this.

"I might be able to," Larry finally admitted. He started pacing, walking back and forth across the lab. It was a motion that seemed familiar to him, something he did a lot of while waiting for this experiment or that to finish cooking. "But it would take years. Years! At such a cost. And whoever has my work might be able to reverse-engineer it. They'd come to the market first."

"And you'd miss your big payout," I said.

Larry nodded, miserable. He was in the habit of counting money that wasn't in his hands yet, the funds that would be accumulating in poor people's accounts over the years.

"Who had access to your lab?" I hadn't committed fully

to taking his case. But I wasn't denying the appeal of finding Larry's thief.

Possibly not to turn them in, but to shake their hand. Or shake them down. It would depend on who had actually done the stealing.

"No one! No one but me," Larry said. "I'm the only one with a key, and I always kept the door padlocked. But this morning, I found that someone had used bolt cutters to remove the lock. They weren't hiding their theft. Not in the least."

That seemed to piss Larry off as much as anything else. If they were going to steal from him, at least be subtle about it?

People were weird.

"Who else knew about what you were brewing back here?"

"All the girls. The models," Larry said. "But I have signed release forms from them. I can give you their names and addresses, as well as before and after photos."

I was impressed. This might not be as bad of a case as I'd thought.

"How many girls?" I asked, doing my own calculations of the fees I was planning on charging good ol' Larry.

"Forty-four, total," Larry said. "Though I think you really only have to focus on the most recent models that I used, as well as only those who received the actual cream, not the placebo."

"While that makes sense, I'm still going to have to look at all of them," I said. "Quickly, just to ensure that they aren't actually going to remain suspects."

Larry gave me a stern look of disapproval, but he said, "Fine."

"Think of it as my own brand of scientific experimentation," I told him. "Eliminate as many suspects as fast as possible, so that you can focus on the productive leads."

Now it was Larry's turn to look impressed. "All right," he said.

We negotiated my fees. I doubled my usual wage, as well as ensuring that he was going to cover all my expenses.

Remember that PITAT? I could already tell that Larry was going to need a big one, recompense for me putting up with him and his whining, in addition to trying to run my investigation for me.

As soon as the money was transferred over, he pulled out copies of all documentation he had, sliding them into a handy, thick envelope. "You'll keep these locked up, right?" he said, holding onto the envelope.

"They'll be safe with me," I said, tugging at it. I hoped I appeared eager to take the case. Or at the very least, eager to start being paid. He couldn't suspect that I'd seen something. Maybe someone in those photos.

"All right," Larry said. "I suppose I should trust you. I've already paid you, and showed you my lab and everything."

"I don't know if you're aware of my reputation," I said.

He gave me a grin. "What, once you're bought, you stay bought?"

"Something like that," I assured him with an easy smile, though the comment stung.

Eventually, I managed to get free of the cold, continuous fans and the hissing distillation. I hurried out of the warehouse district, back to the trains. Of course, my timing was perfect, and I arrived just as the shifts changed. I was sandwiched in on all sides for the rest of the ride back into the city, then into the warrens.

I went directly to my office. The door was still locked, which I knew didn't mean much. But the hair I'd placed on the floor just inside the door hadn't been disturbed. No one had walked through the place while I'd been gone.

I didn't open the envelope until I was seated behind my desk, the door to the office locked again, a glass of cheap whiskey at hand.

I pulled out the releases, paging through the photos until I found the one I'd thought I'd seen earlier.

Jenny Kelmer. Mrs. Kelmer's daughter. She looked enough like her mother that I'd recognized the face when doing a quick scan back at the lab.

Good ol' Larry had been paying her to be one of his models, trying out his vanishing cream, guaranteed to keep the wrinkles away.

So now I had an idea of how she'd managed to save the money to set up her own place, away from her overbearing mother and controlling father.

Seemed like I might have two cases on my hands, though I had no idea how, or even if, they were related.

I spent the rest of the evening going through every photo. I got out a map and plotted out where Larry was finding his models. They appeared to have come from every part of the city, though the later models all came from around the university—Luna U as it was called by the locals.

Was that where Larry had met Jenny? Was I going to have to call Mrs. Kelmer and ask? What were the chances that Mrs. Kelmer had no idea of what her daughter had been involved in?

I was hesitant. I didn't know if Larry was somehow involved in Jenny's disappearance or not.

My gut said the cases were intertwined.

I ignored my gut, at least for now.

The next morning, I stopped by campus, which was also east of the city center, about midway between downtown and the warehouse district. It wasn't anything like an Earth university, with those wonderful ivy-covered walls. Instead, it was assembled out of tan bricks, three stories tall. The roof of the city was even further up, covered in bright lights. If you didn't look closely, you might fool yourself into thinking you were outside.

The buildings took up several city blocks, each its own "quad". While the buildings formed a solid structure looking out on the street, I'd heard rumors of lovely parks just on the other side of the walls, areas where students could gather and learn from one another.

How had Larry gained access? The university was deliberately set up so that the casual visitor couldn't just take a stroll across campus or visit one of those parks. Every door was locked and guarded. And there weren't handy poles or public bulletin boards where Larry could have posted an ad, looking for his models.

Fortunately, I had the address of the building that contained the women's dorm. I was certain it would be the most difficult of them all to assail.

I was also certain that somehow, Larry had stuck his foot into the door there, then refused to leave, like any annoying door-to-door salesman.

I had a plan, though.

I showed up with a messenger cap and a half-dozen roses. They cost me a pretty penny, but I was planning on passing that expense right along to Larry.

I had the names of more than one of the girls who lived there. I had brought a rose for each of them, and had the florist write their names on the tags that were tied to them.

The front area of the dorm reminded me of a federal jail.

I'd seen police offices that looked more friendly and welcoming.

A tall podium overlooked the entire area, inside the door. The matron of the dorm sat on her throne there. No one was going to be able to sneak past her. You were granted access at her whim, and hers alone.

I timed my entrance, coming in just as classes had let out. There were a lot of girls streaming in and out of the dorm. The matron kept her eagle eye on the flow, making sure that only her girls were going in, and no one else.

"Excuse me, ma'am?" I said. I gave her my best "aww shucks" routine. This was when I was thankful for that baby face of mine. "I have a delivery here for Alice, June, Patricia, Jenny, Laverne, and Samantha." I knew that all of the girls resided here, or at least claimed to. I held up the roses so that the matron could see, pointing to the tags.

"I see," the matron said. She had a round face with iron gray hair that she'd pulled back into a severe bun. She didn't wear makeup, and probably didn't approve of the girls who did. Her gray blouse was buttoned up all the way to her double chin and down to her wrists. I would bet that she wore a long, shapeless skirt as well, hiding her legs and ankles.

"You can just leave the flowers here," she pronounced. "I'll make sure that the girls get them."

It wasn't that I didn't trust the old battle ax, but I really needed to see the inside of that dorm, and possibly talk with some of the girls.

"While that sure sounds swell, ma'am, there's a big tip for me if I can actually deliver the flowers to all the girls," I said. "See, they're from Chi-Alpha-Chi. They want to make sure that the girls attend the spring fling next week. And I'm supposed to get their answer when I give them a rose. Not that they won't get the rose if they say no," I assured her.

"You can just find the girls on campus, after their classes," the matron said, waving away my plan.

"But I have to ask them before the other fraternity!" I whined. "Look, I'll split my tip with you!" I slid a ten credit note across her desk.

It was a hefty tip for a delivery boy. But within reason.

As I had suspected, the matron's greedy eyes lit up at the sign of the money. "I will give you ten minutes," she said as her fingers reached for the bill. "If you aren't out of the halls by then, I'm calling campus security."

"Gosh, ma'am, that's not a lot of time," I whined. "Particularly as I don't know the place."

"You'll just have to hurry then, won't you?" she smirked.

I debated if I should try to bribe her with some more money. I knew that she'd be as good as her word. Had possibly already started timing me.

"I'll take it," I told her, giving her a sharp nod. "I can do this."

I figured that might earn me another minute or so, that "can do" attitude.

"Your time starts now," the matron said.

I hurried away, into the bastion of femininity. I had to hand it to good ol' Larry. Wasn't sure how he'd managed to worm his way in here, but whatever scheme he'd tried, it had to be good.

I DON'T KNOW WHAT I WAS EXPECTING. MAYBE MORE pink. More decorations. Certainly more noise or feminine laughter.

Instead, I walked into a sterile hallway. The walls had been painted white, and every speck of dirt was conspicuously swept away at dawn each day. I could smell a small amount of perfume, but these weren't girls who were rich. Or at least didn't smell that way. The floors were plain concrete, and the rugs were as thin as sheets, the red and gold colors faded.

At least a helpful plaque at the entrance gave me a clue which direction I should go, with the higher numbered rooms to the right, the lower ones to the left.

Though I'd paid for all the individual tags on the roses, I wasn't planning on trying to visit all the girls. Particularly not with the matron's time limit.

I checked quickly, and went to the right, visiting rooms one-twenty and one-twenty-eight, without any luck.

The door finally opened at room one-forty. Samantha, who, at least according to the paperwork that Larry had given me, was the next-door neighbor to Jenny Kelmer.

"Yes?" Samantha said as she pulled open the door.

I was instantly struck by just how pretty she was. She had the same sort of coloring I did, pale skin with auburn hair, though she wore hers long and wavy. Cute freckles covered her petite nose, which was completely overshadowed by huge, green eyes. She had the soft curves that a man dreams of, comforting and yet still sexy.

Though the school didn't have a uniform, all the girls I'd seen were dressed similarly enough, in knee-length skirts, knee-high socks, blouses and vests. Samantha's skirt and socks were black, her blouse was white, and her vest was obviously hand knit, done in a green, gold, and red argyle pattern.

I handed her the entire bouquet of roses, along with my card. "I'm here undercover," I told her hurriedly. "I'm actually a private investigator. Can you meet me at The Lazy Cow this afternoon? After your classes?" I said, naming a nearby joint that was frequented by locals and not college kids.

"Uhmm, uhmm, sure," Samantha said. "What's this about?"

"Can't tell you yet. But I suspect foul play," I told her earnestly. "The cops involved aren't doing their job," I added. As there had just been a scandal the previous week about corruption on the police force, it was a believable story.

"Oh. Oh!" Samantha said. She did a quick glance up and down the hallway, making sure that no one was close enough to hear. "I can be there by three."

"Thank you, citizen," I told her seriously. Then I continued in a louder voice. "That sure would be swell if you could deliver the rest of the roses. And make sure that all the girls come to the Chi-Alpha-Chi spring fling!"

"I will," Samantha said with a knowing nod. Then she smiled and winked at me and I skedaddled out of there.

I only had a couple of minutes left. First I walked by the door to Jenny Kelmer's room. I knocked, then tried the door handle. Locked, and no time to try to break in, even with my handy paperclip.

So I walked down the halls, all the way around the quad, before making my way back to the entrance. There was a lovely looking park in the center, and a few of the girls were out there, sitting on blankets as if sunbathing, though it was just the normal lights shining down from the ceiling.

On the far side, I finally found the bulletin board. Larry's ad wasn't on there—it probably had been though, a plain sheet of paper with his name and a phone number, like the one offering tutoring.

So that was how he'd gotten so many models from the campus. Found his first one, then got her to hang his notifications up.

I had to stop thinking of his girls as victims. I didn't have any proof that any of them had run afoul of anything.

Still, I had to wonder where poor Jenny Kelmer had ended up. And if any of it was Larry's fault.

THE LAZY COW TURNED OUT TO BE A JOINT THAT served a huge, heaping breakfast at all times of the day. The chairs and tables were all covered in a cheesy, black and white cloth, supposedly meant to imitate cow hide. Black and white tiles covered the floor, making all the conversations in the room sound tinny. A small counter took up the right of the long, galley-like space, with a set of longhorn horns hung over it. The lights were all bright and cheery, as if to make up for the fact that signs were posted every few feet, warning customers about staying too long.

Seemed they really didn't want college kids hanging out and studying for hours on end.

I ordered coffee and toast, with the "real" honey, though I knew that it was probably just Karo with some food coloring. When Samantha came hurrying in—late, of course—I went to stand with her at the counter and told her to get anything she wanted, on my dime.

Technically, it was Larry's dime, but I wasn't going to share the details on that.

The man running the joint looked askance at Samantha when she first came in, but warmed to her as she ordered eggs, sausage, griddlecakes, and a large glass of milk.

Fortunately, he was happy enough to give me a receipt that I tucked carefully into my wallet. I knew that Larry was going to fight me on every single expense, so I needed good documentation.

Samantha quaffed down the milk as if she were starving. I asked her about her classes, and she was happy to ramble on about them as dish after dish was served.

I must admit, I was impressed at how much food she was able to pack away.

When she finally came up for air after wiping her plate clean, she gave me a sheepish grin. "Sorry," she said. "I know I shouldn't eat so fast! But I have three older brothers, along with two younger squirts, and if you don't finish your plate quickly there are lots of others who will do it for you. Whether you want them to or not."

"I understand," I gave her a huge grin, lying through my teeth. I was an only child, raised by a widow. Or at least that was the story that Mom had always given me, and I'd never wasted my time trying to prove if it was true or not.

"Do you want another glass of milk?" I asked as she looked mournfully down on the empty set of dishes.

"No, thanks, though," Samantha said. She grimaced. "I don't think it's actually milk."

I smiled and nodded. Possibly had seen the inside of a cow at some point. More than likely it had been dried and cut with other things in the meanwhile.

"So, what is this all about?" Samantha finally asked.

I had thought about which case I was supposedly following. I figured I'd start with the one that was at least paying me. "I'm working with Larry Dinklewood," I told her. "Seems that some of his property has gone missing."

"Really?" Samantha breathed out. Her eyes grew wide and she looked at me with surprise.

There was something off about her reaction. I wasn't sure exactly what, though.

"Someone broke into his lab. He had made some additional discoveries, not just the face cream," I lied.

Samantha frowned at that. "The thieves didn't take the new stuff, though, did they? It was just the vanishing cream that they stole, right?"

That confirmed it. Samantha was well aware of the break in, though she hadn't done the deed herself.

"Larry claims they cleaned him out of everything. Even the stuff he was working on for the police," I added.

"The police?" Samantha narrowed her eyes at me. "You mentioned that there was something that the cops weren't investigating."

"That's the second part of my investigation," I admitted. "Jenny Kelmer has gone missing."

"No, that's not possible," Samantha said. "I would swear I saw her at breakfast, just this morning!"

Was Samantha lying? I didn't know her tells well enough to say for certain. "So you've seen her around campus?" I said.

"We don't have any classes together," Samantha said. "But she lives right next to me. I would have noticed if she'd gone missing," she assured me. "She's too conscientious to play hooky. Or if she did, she would have asked me to take notes for her."

"I thought you just said that you didn't share any classes," I pointed out.

Samantha was clearly lying about Jenny and school.

"We used to have classes together, last semester," Samantha maintained. "That was what I meant."

I nodded and let it pass. Samantha seemed truly unconcerned about Jenny.

Wherever Jenny Kelmer was, she was regularly talking with her friends. Just not her mother.

———

By the time Samantha finished telling me about Larry, I had a good idea of how his operation was organized.

The cream really did appear to work, though he was only trying it on younger women as far as she knew.

Why hadn't he tried it on older women? Surely there was a market there. Or did it only work when you had more supple skin to start with?

Larry's experiments seemed legitimate. He was paying everyone for their time, and poor college students really needed the money. He would start out by applying a bit to their forearm, to make sure that there was no discoloration. (She'd heard from one of the other girls that someone's skin had bleached white, and Larry had had to make a big payout to keep the girl from saying anything.) Then he'd move to their hands, just the right, turning the skin soft and supple, before applying any to their face.

On the surface, it appeared that Larry was taking a scientific approach.

To me, it sounded like a scam. Get the clients hooked on the product with just a little bit, before showing what it could really do.

And that was also why he had college students, and not older women.

Get 'em while they were young, train 'em right.

There was only one part of Samantha's ramblings that left me with any new clues. And that was at the very end, when she tried to sell me one of the ribbons she had attached to the strap of her purse.

Seemed that her sorority was raising money for the poor, in particular, those impoverished enough to be forced into the tunnels under the city.

Under the city? In the tunnels?

I gave her a few credits and took one, even if she couldn't give me a receipt. Then she left. I remained, brooding at my table, despite the stinkeye the owner was giving me for staying too long.

There were no homeless people on the Moon, no itinerate hobos or handymen. Central didn't allow those sorts of people up here.

Was that where dear Jenny had gone? On some sort of failed mission of mercy?

Or worse, had she succeeded?

There was only one way to find out. And that was to go down into the tunnels myself.

I wasn't claustrophobic. You couldn't have that condition and live on the Moon. The warrens and lack of open space would get to you, sooner or later.

Still, it was why the windows in my office all bulged out, halfway into the corridor, so that you might fool yourself into thinking that there was more space than there was.

I remembered going to a fancy hotel once, that had been built to Earth scale, with the lobby being two stories tall and fake sunshine pouring through the windows.

Only rich people could afford such space. The next city being built on the Moon, Luna Two as it was appropriately named, was supposed to have domed areas, so people could at least look up at the stars.

Me? I preferred the warrens, that I knew could be closed off automatically in case of a breach.

The tunnels under the city were supposedly cramped. They were for maintenance purposes only, service tunnels. No one was supposed to live there. I'd seen a news reel about it once, some breathless explorer as they made their way down dark, dingy concrete tubes, squawking with surprise at some very well-trained mouse who leaped out, then quickly scurried away, back to their warm cage.

Central assured us that there weren't actually any mutants

living under the city, despite the fact that everyone knew about them. That was primarily the reason behind the fake documentary, to show that no mutants lived there.

I knew better. I may have had too much to drink the night I saw them. No one believed me when I tried talking about them. I got the hint quickly that trying to expose the mutants would get shut down hard.

Now, I was wondering about the poor who Samantha and the others were convinced lived there.

Central again maintained that they provided housing for one and all. No one lived in the tunnels—no Humans. While I didn't believe Central when it came to the mutants, I had believed them in terms of the regular, everyday Joe.

Which was the lie? Which was the truth?

I didn't want to find out, but I was going to have to.

THERE WASN'T ANY EASY WAY TO GET INTO THE TUNNELS under the cities, no clear stairway marked "no entrance" or a mere security guard to slip past.

No, the way down into the tunnels was through the equivalent of one of the "sewer" grates that graced the floor of every train station.

They were all easy to see. Everyone knew about them.

But they were difficult to access. The train stations were always busy.

Which stopped foolhardy kids from breaking into the tunnels during the day.

It wouldn't stop them at night though, say, around three AM, after the last of the bar rush was over.

I had looked into the charity that Samantha was supposedly raising money for. They had a soup kitchen close to the east-side station. None of their official literature mentioned poor people in tunnels.

Was that just something Samantha had made up? It was too specific a detail for a throwaway line.

But if there were poor people in the tunnels, coming back up into the city on the east side, close to the warehouse district, using one of the least busy train stations would make sense.

Two other people got off at the station with me at that three AM hour, a pair of laborers who were putting in overtime at the warehouses. They quickly were on their way, leaving me with a supposedly busted shoelace in the empty station.

While riding in a mostly empty train hadn't bothered me, the echoing, open space did.

Guess I was more used to being surrounded by people than I'd realized.

The station, like all of them, wasn't fancy. It wasn't for rich people, but for poor working schmucks. It was merely a square opening carved into the tunnel wall. White tiles lined the edges, with the name of the station done in black tile. Both the floor and the walls were gray concrete, reinforcing the carved rock. Stairs at the back led to the street above.

Unlike the Earth trains, no one had to buy a ticket to ride a lunar train. Central operated them out of our taxes, and I was mostly happy to pay them to do it. So there were no guards or gates at the entrance.

The manhole going down to the tunnels was off to the side, tucked into a corner. It looked heavy, made out of solid iron with the initials LSAP (Lunar Sewer and Power) embossed around the edge.

For a moment, I regretted not bringing a crowbar or something solid to lift the cover. But once I got closer, I discovered that there were fingerholes drilled into the top, right under the letter L. When I poked my fingers through, they brushed against dark cloth that had been taped to the underside, so no light would shine through from below.

I hesitated. That was pretty solid evidence that someone (or if it was the mutants, something) was regularly climbing in and out of this hole.

Did I really want to go down there alone?

I did have my handy ray gun tucked into my jacket pocket. While I was licensed to carry it, I never flashed it about. Didn't want anyone taking too close a look at it, or the fact that I'd had Doc down at the pawn shop soup it up so that it was now powerful enough to stun a bull.

I heard the next train speeding my way, the electric motors whining.

It was now or never.

I slipped my fingers back into the roughly drilled holes, drawing up the cover. The rank smell made me wrinkle my nose as I pulled the cover over my head with a solid *thunk*.

My mother had always told me that my incessant curiosity would be the death of me yet.

And who knows? One of these years, she might be proven right. Not that she had the wherewithal to know it. She barely recognizes me when I go to visit.

I stayed where I was, just under the manhole cover, clinging to the metal ladder. I took shallow breaths, as the smell of sewage filled the area.

But it wasn't completely dark. I'd come equipped with a large flashlight, just in case. However, lights shone below me.

I could do this. I slowly climbed down the ladder. My foot stuck down into open air at the end. I continued going down, using just my arms. Good thing I kept myself in fit enough shape chasing down leads and never eating enough.

Finally, I figured I could just drop the last few feet, into the smooth, round tunnel, obviously bored by one of the automatic tunnel makers.

I didn't stand right back up. The tunnel was about five and a half feet across, and about that tall, as well. I only had to bend my neck to keep my head from hitting rock. There wasn't any water running down the tunnel—wastes got flushed using jets of air. So where was that smell coming from?

I decided to follow my nose, as one direction of the tunnel looked identical to the other. About ten feet away I saw an access hatch, leading to a much smaller space.

The actual sewage tunnels.

They weren't as big as the one I stood in, perhaps only a couple of feet across. I heard the *boom* of air from my right, and watched through the glass as a mass of waste glided by.

Seemed the maintenance tunnels were just that—man-sized so someone could come down and fix the sewer line if necessary.

I continued my stroll along the tunnel, not finding anything but regular cleanouts for the sewer line that ran parallel. Where were the mutants? Or the poor, for that matter? No one was camped out in this tunnel, at least as far as I could see.

There must be another hatchway, one that I'd missed. Or it was in the other direction.

I slowed my pace and turned back. Even though I didn't need it, I got out my flashlight and played the beam along the floor, walls, and ceiling, trying to catch a glimpse of a catch or hidden compartment.

Finally found it on the other side of where I'd first come down, about ten feet along. A seam in the smooth wall, one that I wouldn't have seen if I hadn't been looking for it. Took a bit to find the next fingerholds, up along the ceiling.

All I had to do was push on them, and the wall folded back on itself smoothly on invisible hinges.

The scent that whooshed out was worse than the sewer smell that had lingered in the tunnel.

Much worse.

Well, that would just mean a dry cleaning bill that good ol' Larry could pick up.

I stepped through the dark opening, and into another world.

WHILE THE TUNNELS THEMSELVES WERE DRY AND brightly lit, this place was dark and humid. I stood on the platform at the top of a set of black steel stairs leading down.

The door closed behind me automatically. I played the flashlight on the seam, finding and memorizing where the fingerholds were in case I needed to get out in a hurry.

Then I killed the light, giving myself time for my eyes to adjust. The cavern that I stood in was huge as far as I could tell. Much bigger than any of the parks up in the city. The air was moist against my skin, thick and heavy. I felt as though I'd stepped into a luxury spa, the kind that offered actual showers with water.

I knew that Mars had hidden oceans. Did the Moon as well? What else was Central hiding from us?

Someone far below me was talking. Or perhaps singing. I quietly made my way down the staircase, holding onto the slimy cold handle as I went deeper. The smell increased, something wet and rotting, a scent I'd never smelled before and couldn't wait to get out of.

The staircase went on and on, at least five full flights. I was sure hoping like hell that I never had to try to escape and run up them.

By the time I reached the bottom, I could see fairly well. The lights weren't electric but some sort of luminous substance growing on the walls, giving off an eerie, purplish illumination. I heard what sounded like chanting going on to my right, growing louder as I moved forward.

While I wasn't claustrophobic, I sure as hell didn't like all this open space around me. It just wasn't right for a warren kid like me. I'd heard about other Moon rats who'd hated the Earth the first time they'd visited. All that open air and wind.

Wind meant a breach up here.

I found myself crouching down as I went ahead, as if making myself less of a target to whatever unseen monster was hidden above me, in all that space. I didn't want to think about huge spiders spinning webs or blood-sucking bats resting in the corners.

Didn't take long to get to edge of the stage where the singing was going on.

There, I found sweet Jenny Kelmer. She wore a long white gown, and a single spotlight shone down on her angelic form, lighting up her golden hair. In front of her, a mass of monsters celebrated together in worship. The chanting came from the crowd, in grunts and growls, not really in any language.

A long line of supplicants stood in front of Jenny. One by one, the mutants came forward for their blessing.

They weren't as ugly as they sounded, but I wouldn't want to meet any of them in a dark alley. They tended to have long, pale faces, with jagged teeth and no noses. Their hands were clawlike, and they wore mere rags over their distorted bodies. Tumors grew in abundance across their skin, sticking up like a second head from the neck of one, or sprouting like mushrooms across the back of another.

They came up to Jenny, then knelt. That was when I

realized just how tall they all were, the shortest being at least six feet tall, and the bigger monsters over eight feet.

It appeared that Jenny had tamed them. She slathered a bluish lotion on their upturned faces, good ol' Larry's fountain of youth, if I had to guess.

And it worked miracles, just as Larry had said it would.

As each supplicant turned away from Jenny, before they ambled off the stage, I would catch a glimpse of their faces. How Human they appeared to be. How their eyes rose up, and instead of dark holes their sockets now had color and intelligence hiding behind them.

The effect wasn't permanent, of course. Just a breath of sanity before the monster returned.

While those still waiting in line were the ones chanting, it was the rest, those who'd had their turn at playing Human, who were growling. Cat-calling. Rumbling with despair.

Jenny was still up on stage playing savior, not realizing that her flock was about to turn against her.

How had she made the connection? Had she been doing some mad science on her own, stealing a little of Larry's special cream for her friends down here?

I debated leaving her to her just deserts. It would serve her right for those she'd been trying to save to bring her down.

She was merely a girl, though. Raised in a stifling environment. Had probably been thrilled when she realized that she could actually make a difference.

She didn't understand just how dangerous it was to give someone, even a monster, false hope.

I waited in the shadows on the edge of the stage. The crowd was growing restless. Only a few remained in the supplicants' line. The hymns they'd been chanting before grew sketchy, the sound drowned out by the fierce wails that now sometimes arose from the crowd, as the monstrous nature of an individual returned after their too-brief visit to sanity.

One of those waiting couldn't stand it any longer. He was one of the bigger beasts. Tumors grew across his shoulders, giving him the appearance of a linebacker. Scraggly silver hair clung to the edges of his skull. Horrid mewling sounds came from his mouth as he rushed the stage.

He pushed back the few still standing in line. Though he couldn't speak words, his intention was obvious. He wanted more of the magical cream. Right now.

"No, no, I can't, I'm sorry," Jenny said. She must have had some sort of actress training, as her words echoed out across the entire audience. "More right now will not help. You need to be patient."

The monster raised his head to the ceiling and roared, a deep, ugly tone. It raised all the hackles along the back of my neck and had me reaching for my ray gun.

"No!" Jenny said firmly. She put her hands behind her back, as if hiding the jar of magical ointment would stop this thing.

She wasn't playing keep away from a bratty cousin.

The monster screamed again.

Some of the other mutants around him tugged at him, trying to pull him back, get him to leave Jenny alone.

The ease with which he shrugged them off, throwing one of them all the way across the stage and dumping him onto the rest of the audience, was truly impressive.

As well as frightening.

Jenny finally seemed to realize that she might be in danger. The monster stalked toward her, intent on either stealing the jar and using it all up on himself, or smothering himself in her blood. It was kind of hard to tell which he wanted more at that time.

I knew that it would be stupid to rush into this, to pull a stupid knight-in-shining-armor routine.

I also knew that I didn't have any choice.

I shot the monster fully in the chest with my ray gun.

The first cone of blue light only appeared to tickle him. He growled and tried to shove it away, as if it were little better than a gnat bite.

I flipped the switch on the handle to up the amperage.

This time, I got the monster's attention. He screamed as he stumbled back.

I jumped up onto the stage, grabbing Jenny's hand. "Time to go," I told her, trying to pull her back toward the edge of the stage.

I really was *not* looking forward to racing up all those stairs. But that was the only way I knew that led out of this place.

Jenny resisted me. Of course. She still didn't have any idea of the danger she was facing.

"I can't leave the other vials behind!" Jenny said, reaching back.

"Leave them," I said.

"But they'll go crazy! Use them all up!" Jenny complained.

I looked back to where Jenny was pointing. She still had half a dozen bottles of glowing blue cream.

"What a great idea," I told her.

I let go of her hand and picked up a vial.

Big, dumb, and already injured was struggling to get to his feet, to come at me again.

"Here you go, big fella," I said, lobbing a jar directly at him.

It was a miracle that he caught it. But the howl of delight once he realized what he had turned more than a few heads his direction.

Which was exactly what I had hoped.

"Here! Here! Catch!" I said as I lobbed jars out into the audience below the stage.

The monsters converged on the poor suckers who'd managed to snag their prize.

Which meant that Jenny and I could get away *without* having to race up all those damned stairs.

I still ended up blasting a few of the mutants, who thought that maybe they still needed Jenny, to get them out of our way . I even picked up a souvenir along the way, a hunk of mutant skin. But for the most part, the rest of the crowd ignored us and fell on one another, based on the screeches of outrage and the howls of pain.

Jenny was crying all the way back to the top. "Those poor, poor people," she wept.

"They aren't people," I told her as I pressed my fingers against the hidden latch and the door slid open. "Not any longer."

"But they could be people again," Jenny reasoned as I shoved her in front of me, out into the service tunnel.

"Do you know that for certain?" I said. "Have you had any success changing one completely?"

"No, but if I'd only had a little more time—"

"It never would have worked," I said, hustling her down the service tunnel, back toward the manhole cover leading up to the city.

I wasn't about to fall to my knees and kiss the dirty floor when I made it topside. I may have considered it.

"Oh, what do you know?" Jenny said crossly as she followed me up out of the tunnels and back into the train station.

Warren, sweet warren.

"What do I know? I know people, that's what I know," I told her. I was a little short tempered at that point. Hadn't slept in too long and still reeked of the sewers and those who lived in them. "Your pal, good ol' Larry? He never would have created a cream that had a permanent effect. His plan was to get rich. The only way to do that is to create a concoction that leaves 'em begging for more."

Jenny grew very quiet as that, waiting beside me as the train pulled up. The first of the warehouse workers rolled off. I had a story all ready, about being at a fancy dress party and having to go on a scavenger hunt, if any cops did think to question why we were dressed as we were, smelling like we did.

"So I don't suppose his notes are going to do anyone any good either, are they?" Jenny said quietly after we'd both snagged a seat.

"Not a damned bit," I told her. Despite her dark look, I wasn't about to apologize for swearing.

"What will you do now?" I said after a few moments of stony silence.

"I suppose I could go back to school," Jenny said with a bitter laugh. "Go back to being Daddy's Perfect Princess."

"Look, I get it. You're just trying to do some good in the world," I said. "But there are other ways to go about it."

Jenny nodded, still miserable over her failure.

She'd thought she was going to save the world, or at the very least, an entire people.

She'd get over it.

"There are volunteer organizations," I told her.

"Charities I could run. Yes, I get it," Jenny said with a worldly sigh.

We rode in silence for a few more moments before she finally said, "Thank you for helping me."

I was fairly shocked. I hadn't expected her to thank me at all.

"You're welcome."

She got off at the station closest to the campus, and I took the long ride back to my own empty flat. One room, with a Murphy bed and a party line coming into the building. I cleaned up, ate a tuna sandwich over the sink before I laid down and tried to sleep.

Would Jenny call her parents finally? I expected she would, as her grand scheme hadn't worked. Maybe she'd be able to get her father to finance some monster outreach program or something.

I dreamed of wide open spaces, completely empty of all people, leaving me drenched in a puddle of sweat. Made me thankful for loud, obnoxious neighbors for once.

GOOD OL' LARRY DIDN'T WANT TO BELIEVE ME THAT A mutant had broken into his lab. But then I showed him the piece of skin that I'd blown off the hide of one of them. He held it between his fingers, caressing it.

I didn't like the wheels that I saw turning in his head. Then again, it wasn't any of my business.

We settled up quickly. He actually paid all my expenses without me having to threaten him with violence more than twice.

Mrs. Kelmer stopped by the office the next day, wanting to thank me profusely for saving her daughter. She wasn't sure what crazy religious cult had nabbed her in the first place, but Jenny appeared to be seeing straight at last.

"You're welcome," I told Mrs. Kelmer, more than once, before I finally got her shoved out the door and went back to the peace and quiet of my office.

Sure, I liked being alone. Working alone. But I lived in the heart of the warrens. There were people all around me.

On all sides. All the time. That was what I was used to. What I'd grown up with.

I couldn't imagine those wide open spaces down below the tunnels of the city. What it must be like to be living out in the open, without a solid roof directly overhead.

No wonder they'd all turned into monsters.

I CAUGHT THE NEWS LATER THAT NIGHT, WHEN I'D BEEN sitting at a local bar nursing a glass of good whiskey. Seemed the cops had performed a raid on an illegal lab located in the warehouse district.

I knew Larry would blame me. But he'd been right the first time. Once bought, I stayed bought. It had probably been Jenny in a fit of pique.

Still, I couldn't help but wonder what had happened to those notes she'd stolen, who she'd given them to. Was there another mad scientist's lab working on a cure for the mutants? Or that fountain of youth, as Larry had described it?

Who knew what other weird and wild experiments were going on, right under our noses? We all knew that science could go too far.

How long before we would be proven right?

[3]

THE CASE OF THE MISSING TWIN

I WAS NEVER ATTRACTED TO MEN. DIDN'T SEE ANY HARM in it—love and let love, that was what I said. I prefer a woman's curves and soft sighs, that sweet smell of perfume. Not as though I was experiencing any of that on a regular basis, but a guy could dream, right?

I knew my chances were low, though. I lived on the Moon in Luna City, underground, where the ratio of men to women was at least two to one according to Central's statistics. Might have been higher—I'd never bothered to count noses, and it wouldn't have been the first time that Central had misled the public. Wouldn't be the last either.

It was the middle of a Friday afternoon and I didn't have much going on. All right, I didn't have *anything* going on, no cases, no suspects to follow, no evidence to be gathered. I'd already read all the papers, even the letters to the editor section which were written by the common man, that is, idiots.

I'd considered closing up shop early, except that there wasn't anywhere to go. I wasn't flush enough to go out drinking, and I didn't feel like going back to my one room apartment, either.

I could always go to a "park"—though that much wide open space generally unnerved a warren rat like me. There was still solid rock up above, with cleverly placed lights in the high ceiling that shone down like sunlight. Some of the fancier places had artificial grass, though no trees. Couldn't afford to water them, not someplace as dry as the Moon.

There wasn't anything in the office to fix up. I had a watercooler in the corner, quietly burbling to itself. The fan in the center of the ceiling was more for looks than to actually push around the stale air pumped in by Central. I kept the blinds over the windows behind me closed—who wanted to see the waves of factory workers crammed into the corridor when shift changed? The notes I kept in the two filing cabinets were already filed and strictly alphabetical.

I may not have been the best detective on the Moon, Venus, or Mars, no matter what the jingle in my ad said, but I kept damned good notes. Even on the cases that were so outrageous that no one would ever believe the truth.

Therefore, I was grateful when I heard a quiet knock on the door. "Come in!" I called cheerily, pushing the newspapers to one side of my big berth of a desk.

I could barely believe my eyes when I saw the guy who came walking in. He was the most beautiful man I'd ever seen. Flawless black hair that probably looked good when it was mussed, as opposed to my own wild coppery curls that would frizz if I ever let them grow long. He had keen green eyes that practically shone, even from across the room. They gave him a piercing, intelligent gaze. His nose was a little sharp, but that was in perfect contrast to his full, sensual lips. He had a cleft in the center of his chin and a strong jaw. His skin was a shade darker than mine but still the white of a lunar warren rat.

Now, as I said, I'm not attracted to men. However, if there was ever anyone who might get me interested in batting for the other team, this guy would be the one.

I found myself standing up, automatically buttoning my suit jacket and smoothing it out. Did I look all right? Was I presentable enough?

I really wanted to make this man my client. Even if I'd had four other cases going simultaneously, I'd still want to take him on.

"Good afternoon," I said, striding around my desk, my hand already out to shake his.

"Hello," the man said.

He had a striking tenor voice, higher than I'd expected, but it suited him perfectly.

"I'm Alvin Goodfellow," I told him. I made myself release his hand, shocked at my own behavior.

No dame had ever made me get out of my chair that fast. Something was going on. I found my own suspicious mind starting to wonder at my reaction.

"I'm Peter Bryant, but you can call me Pete," he said. His smile was charming and warm, though I could detect a hint of anxiety at the corners.

"Alvin," I told him. "Not Al." I hated being called "Al."

I made myself turn away from Pete and go sit in my own chair, on the far side of my desk, instead of hitching a hip up and staying closer to him.

I had to get myself under control, put distance between us. I still didn't know what was going on. I pulled out a notebook and resolved to write absolutely everything down, as I was pretty sure my memory of this meeting wasn't going to be accurate in the least.

"So how can I help you, Pete?" I said.

He gave me a bemused smile, as if he understood the

game I was playing with myself. "Someone has been impersonating me," he said.

I blinked, surprised. There were two men with such stunning good looks on the Moon? Could that even be possible?

Did that mean he might have a sister as well?

Questions for another time.

"How do you know? What has this imposter done?" I said. I made myself take a deep breath. I was already believing him and willing to go that extra mile for this man. I needed to slow down.

"At first, it was little things. People at the grocery store would ask me what I'd forgotten, as if they'd already seen me that day, picking up things," Pete said.

I nodded and wrote down almost everything he said verbatim. People mistaking him for someone else just didn't seem likely. I wasn't ready to believe him. Or so I told myself.

After I finished my notes I looked up, expectant.

"Then yesterday," Pete continued, "I went to my post office box only to find that someone had picked up my mail. Agnes—the woman behind the counter—swore that I'd already been in that day."

"That's strange," I said, though it still wasn't enough to convince me. The woman who sat behind the counter at my post office was blind as a bat. Until she'd been put on the front desk, she'd frequently mixed up what few letters I received, putting them into someone else's slot, unable to actually read the address. "Anything else?"

I couldn't interpret the look Pete gave me. Quizzical, I'd have to guess, as if he'd thought that just those two incidents should be enough to incite me to action.

"The worst was today," Pete finally admitted. "When I went to the bank to deposit my paycheck, I found out that half my account had been drained!" He shook his head, his mobile lips set in a frown. "The bank manager swore up and down that I'd been the one who'd been in. They even showed me the withdrawal slip. Whoever it was has been practicing my penmanship, because the signature was identical to mine."

"Interesting," I said. That really was damning. "Which bank?"

"Far Brothers Permanent Building Society," Pete said.

That made me raise my eyebrows. That was a pretty fancy private bank. Doubted the security guard would even let me in the door. Its headquarters was north of downtown, as if holding itself aloof from the rest of the financial district. I'd read about the bank just that afternoon. It was one of the primary financers of Luna Two, the new city that they had yet to break ground on but that everyone was already talking about.

Central was planning on putting big domes over Luna Two, if it ever got built. Wasn't someplace I was looking forward to going. I'd much rather have warrens with bulkheads that could be closed if there was ever a breach. I'd never trust something like a dome, no matter how "new and improved" the NuGlass supposedly was.

"When was the withdrawal made?" I asked. May as well start digging into the details of this case because I knew I'd be taking it. Particularly if there really was someone else as good looking as Pete out there.

"Last week," Pete said. "Thursday, the twelfth."

I counted back. Eight days before. "Was that when people at the grocery store started commenting on you coming back for things?"

Pete thought about it for a moment. "No, I think that started a couple of days beforehand."

I wrote down the tenth as the possible appearance day of the imposter. It gave me something to go on. Though it might have been the ninth as well, which would have been a Monday.

"And I take it you don't have any brothers or sisters?" I said. Figured it wouldn't hurt to ask that as part of the case. Not that I'd plan on tracking down any siblings, in particular, female siblings.

Pete shook his head. "No. Only child. And I wasn't born here on the Moon. I was recruited just out of college and immigrated then. Mom and Dad swear that there were never any siblings. I have some cousins, but they're supposedly all still on Earth."

I didn't show any regret that Pete had no sisters. I'd have to follow up on the cousins at some point, though I doubted that any of them could be as perfect as Pete.

"Where do you work? Has the imposter shown up there at all?"

"No, thank god," Pete said. He gave a mirthless chuckle. "I work at Homonym Laboratory. If the imposter had gotten through the security there…I don't know what I would have done."

"I see," I said, though I was going to have to do some more research. As far as I knew, Homonym Labs made women's face cream that was supposed to reverse aging. Since I'd had cases in the past that involved such products, I knew a little about the company, but not much.

Maybe they had some gels that worked, which had given this man his beauty.

"So why come to me, and not the police?" I said. It was a question I always asked. Better to find out at the start just how far outside the law a case might lead me.

"I did go to the police," Pete said.

The scowl he gave seemed inappropriate on that face of his. Smiles and intense concentration were much better suited. It helped break the spell. Either that, or my natural cynicism was reasserting itself.

"They refused to help, said I didn't have enough of a case," Pete continued. "They actually accused me of manufacturing the evidence that I had so far. When I showed them the withdrawal slip, they said it was a fake. No one could copy someone's signature so perfectly."

I raised an eyebrow at that. Of course, it didn't surprise me that the police could be that arrogant. However, I knew more than one forger who was that good.

I asked Pete about his routine, where he generally went and when. It seemed he worked almost all the time, locked in that laboratory of his, though he wouldn't talk about the work he did, saying it was confidential.

I didn't press. I knew I should have. But I wanted to see the smile back on his face, not the frown.

I noted down all the details, trying to piece together his life. He had friends—most people other than me did. But they'd not met the imposter.

Why had the imposter gone to the same grocery store as Pete? Was this other man, Pete 2, testing the perfection of his disguise? The ultimate test hadn't been at the bank. Pete wouldn't have gone there too often, maybe once a month to deposit his paycheck.

Pete left me a copy of the withdrawal slip, then we said our goodbyes. I told him I'd contact him on Monday to let him know if I'd found out anything over the weekend.

Not that I'd be working through the weekend. Not even for him. Really.

After Pete had gone, I stayed seated in my chair, musing at my reaction to this man. Why was I so drawn to him? There had to be something else, not just the perfection of his features.

I was glad I'd taken such good notes, as I didn't

remember the specifics of our conversation, just the tone of his voice, the play of his sensual lips.

I would think he'd have a difficult time getting anything done if women had the same reaction to him as I had. He looked fully Human, but I had to wonder if somehow there was a gene or two from the warriors of Mars, who were said to take not just female lovers but male as well.

Whatever it was, I knew I had to be extra careful in this case. I was going to have to question ever conclusion I came to, every fact I discarded as irrelevant.

At the same time, I found myself wanting to get started, to do something, anything, to put that smile back on Pete's face.

Yup. This was going to be a tricky case. Maybe my hardest yet.

I still couldn't wait to get started.

FIRST THING I DID WAS TO GO TO THE LIBRARY TO LOOK up Homonym Laboratories. I loved the downtown library. I didn't come here often—the elderly woman who ran the place, Mrs. Thornton, didn't approve of freeloaders like me coming in and reading the newspapers when I could afford to buy my own. She had weird criteria for judging whether she felt you were worthy of using her resources.

The library ran all along one end of a big block just south of downtown. The building was a single story and took up the entire short side of the block. Floor to ceiling windows looked out over the street on three sides, as the fourth was connected to the office buildings next door.

Faux brick faced the building—sheets of rubber made out to look like rough brownish-red bricks with off-white mortar running between them. It wasn't until you touched it that you realized it was fake. That, and it had a faint rubbery scent.

The entrance was on the south side of the building and took up most of that edge. Huge concrete lion statues stood guard on either side of the brass doors. I remembered one Christmas some mook had dared to put red-and-white-striped scarves around their necks. While most people had laughed at the pictures in the newspapers and thought it was cute, the battle-ax running the library had nearly come unhinged.

So now, people were constantly adding decorations to the lions. I'd seen green feathered boas, white fur stoles, necklaces made out of beads as well as flowers. Today, they were each sporting a rather lovely garland of fake green pine boughs.

I knew the picturesque scene wouldn't last. As soon as Mrs. Thornton realized that her statues were decorated again, she'd come and tear them off. Rather a shame.

I nodded to both lions before I made my way through the wide, brass doors. Seemed only right to acknowledge their finery before it was destroyed.

Right inside the door stood the huge round information desk. Though the room behind it was open and echoing, barely a sound could be heard. Mrs. Thornton's iron fist made sure that everyone who entered her domain behaved decorously. The smell of paper dominated the space, a pulpy smell that even a fresh newspaper didn't bring.

"Yes, young man?" Mrs. Thornton said, peering down at me from her perch. She had iron gray hair pulled back so tightly into a bun that the skin of her face was drawn back and pinched. Dark sullen eyes stared out over high cheekbones. Her nose was large and got into everyone's business. Her most natural expression was a scowl, which she regularly treated me with.

I didn't know how old Mrs. Thornton was, but I was no

spring chicken myself, not a great catch at thirty-five and still single, married to my job. Still, I tried not to take offence at her greeting.

"I need some information about Homonym Laboratories," I told her.

Though she might not have favored me, I did usually come in with unusual requests. I suspected that was why she tolerated me most of the time.

"Are you looking for encyclopedia information, such as the history of the company?" Mrs. Thornton inquired. "Or their current product line?" Her tone implied that my original statement had been far too sloppy for someone of her ilk to take seriously.

I didn't see how learning about the past of the company would help me. Then again, I was interested in their incorporation papers. Were they a public company? Did they have shareholders to whom they paid dividends?

I reframed my inquiry. "I'd like to see the business side of the company," I said. "Incorporation papers, stock certificates, product lines."

Mrs. Thornton just glared at me. "Legal documents are not kept here, Alvin Goodfellow, as you well know. Those are stored at the courthouse. All I can give you is the history as well as list of current products."

That surprised me, actually. I had expected her to have more information than that. "I'll take those, then."

"Fine," she said. She wrote down my request and slipped it into one of the tubes that ran from her station to the circulation desk at the back. Many of the books were kept behind locked gates, as Mrs. Thornton didn't want "riffraff" to be thumbing through her precious books without a dedicated purpose.

The paper was quickly sucked up by the vacuum system and sent winging to the back desk.

"Thank you," I told her, trying to be more gracious than she was.

"If you ever want a *real* case to solve, you'd figure out who keeps defacing my lions," Mrs. Thornton said, her tone still disapproving.

I actually had a very good idea who it was, though it probably wasn't a single culprit. Instead, I figured it would be every person in the neighborhood who Mrs. Thornton disapproved of.

"I'll try to remember that, the next time I have some downtime," I told her lightly, though there was no way in hell I'd take a sucker bet like that. Plus, she wouldn't pay me anything, and my time was worth the money I charged.

Even with Pete's cute face, I'd still insisted on triple my usual amount. He'd tried half-heartedly to bargain me down, but I could tell his heart wasn't in it. It was as if he wanted to pay me, to give me the money.

Behind the information desk the room opened up. Islands of tall metal shelves filled with popular fiction books took up much of the space. To the left, close to the windows, uncomfortable metal chairs and tables were spread out, as well as the wooden stand the newspapers were hung from. The hard vinyl floor cushioned some of the sounds, though it was still an empty, echoing space. Not a speck of dust was suffered to exist, even in the corners.

The back wall was made out of cinder blocks painted a somber brown, probably meant to convey the seriousness of the place but only succeeded in making it drab. An open window was cut out of the center, lighted from behind, like a cloakroom at a fancy theatre.

Behind the wall all the reference and non-fiction books were stashed, enclosed on shelves with metal gates keeping them locked in tight. I'd always thought about breaking in here some night, just to see what Mrs. Thornton had hidden back there.

Maybe the next time I wasn't working too hard…though I knew I'd never actually do it. That was a bridge too far.

The back desk was staffed by a Mrs. Thornton wannabe —Linda McMurphy. She might have been pretty, once. She'd started to emulate Mrs. Thornton's hairstyle, pulling her thick blonde hair back into a severe bun. Her face was rounder and her cheeks softer than her mentor's. There was still time for her to save herself, though I doubted she wanted to. She was determined to take over the entire library and run it with as tight of an iron fist as Mrs. Thornton.

I suppose it was good to have some ambition in life.

She primly handed me the books that Mrs. Thornton had requested. I nodded my thanks to her rather than trying to engage her in conversation. She had an even sharper tongue than the head librarian, and had been mortally offended the one time I'd invited her to have coffee with me.

It wasn't that I was trying to save her. I couldn't save myself. I was trying to be nice to her, though, figuring that I might be able to get some favors, sweet talk her into giving me access to more of those books, other than the ones Mrs. Thornton prescribed as suitable for me.

Probably, others had tried that game before, possibly taken advantage of her. She was deeply suspicious now, and wouldn't even say hello.

I took the two thick volumes she handed me across the space to one of the empty tables in the corner.

The first book turned out to be a history of all the prominent companies on the Moon. It didn't surprise me that the book was published by Central. The book would be used as propaganda, sent to other industries to try to get them to set up headquarters on the Moon as well.

I learned that Homonym Laboratories had been one of

the first companies on the Moon. Huh. That struck me as odd, particularly for a company that specialized in women's face cream. The first few waves of Loonies (as they were called back in the day) had all been men.

What struck me was the company's vision statement—Dedicated to Making a More Perfect You.

That had certainly been the case with Pete, who was one of the most perfect individuals I'd ever met. At least in terms of looks, I had to remind myself. I'd only just met the man. I really didn't have a good handle on his personality yet.

The labs were a privately held company and it appeared they had no intention of ever going public, at least according to this book. Board of directors were mostly located on Earth, with only a few up here on the Moon.

I put that book to the side and picked up the second one. Surprisingly, it was a book published by the patent office of some of the more important chemical patents that had been granted over the past five years.

Homonym Laboratories had acquired quite a few. The chemistry was way over my head. But in addition to the skin tonics that guaranteed elasticity, and the bronzing lotions for acquiring that perfect tan, they'd also been granted quite a few patents for duplication of materials.

Since the materials themselves were natural, they couldn't be granted any sort of patent on that. However, the process of chemical reproduction was quite complicated.

As I said, the technical details and math were far beyond me. But one word stuck out, a word I wasn't familiar with.

Clone.

Mrs. Thornton did keep a huge dictionary out where the common public could use it to better educate themselves. It was open on a sturdy wooden pedestal toward the front of the open room. The book itself was massive, at least three feet tall and wide, and probably a foot and a half thick. The paper was onion-skin thin. It smelled of dark ink and hidden secrets.

A magnifying glass was attached to the pedestal on a long brass chain. I used that to peer at the text as the printing was so small.

The word came from the Greek, meaning an offshoot of a plant, something that was identical to its parent.

Chills ran across my shoulders and down my spine as I thought of the implications.

Had Homonym Laboratories made Pete the best version of himself? Then created a clone of that perfection? Without telling the original?

And how was I to go about proving it?

I'd told myself that I wasn't going to be working this case on the weekend. However, since I really didn't have anything better to do, I figured what the hell.

Besides, the fee I was charging Pete was surely enough to justify my time.

Saturday morning found me waiting outside Pete's doorstep. No, not with a rose in hand or some such nonsense. I had a paper in front of my face, leaning against the wall of a nearby shop.

Pete lived in apartments that were much nicer than my bachelor rooms. Families lived in these sorts of places, as well as young couples with careers. Most of the other tenants in my building were factory workers, which meant the flats were cheap and small.

The apartments in Pete's building were much larger. The ones on the third floor, built into the roof, probably had three bedrooms in addition to an actual living room and kitchen. At least they weren't fancy enough to have a doorman—those residences were closer to downtown.

As it was Saturday, there weren't waves of workers on their way into their offices, but just a few families out strolling, making their way to the parks and nearby restaurants. I had been concerned about Pete spotting me. He didn't appear to notice me as he hurried by, on his way to the train station just up the street.

I followed nonchalantly behind him. If he was always this unaware of his surroundings, there was no wonder that his imposter had been able to easily ascertain Pete's schedule.

The train station here wasn't much better than any of the others, just three staircases leading down to an opening where the train would appear and disappear. As all public transportation was free, there weren't any ticket takers or guards.

I rode in the car behind Pete, who read his newspaper like the other men on the train. A little girl and her mother watched me with big eyes from where they were seated. Given the girl's fancy red dress, matching hat, as well as white stockings and patent leather shoes, I assumed they were off on some sort of family visit.

Which reminded me that I needed to go and visit my own dear mother before the end of the month. Just one more stone around my neck, weighing me down.

I wasn't surprised that the station where Pete departed the train was in the factory district. I assumed that his laboratory had some sort of chemical plant associated with it. The book I'd looked at the day before had just listed the corporate offices, which were located downtown. They hadn't bothered with the actual laboratory address. I mean, who cared about the place where the actual work was getting done?

Tall buildings crowded around the entrance to the train station. Many of them were huge—a single building taking up an entire block—and had no facing to hide the dusty moon rock they were built out of. Few had lights in the windows, probably more for security than because they had any workers there that day.

Still, Pete and I weren't completely alone on the street. Instead of workers, it was managers who appeared to be hurrying off to their offices, probably trying to catch up on that very important paperwork that the factory owners insisted on.

None of them nodded to Pete as he walked by. Either everyone was in a hurry, or Pete was actively frowning, keeping people at a distance.

I didn't see any covert glances following him along, no one trying to get close enough to chat.

Did his beauty only work sometimes? Or was it just me who was so susceptible?

Homonym Laboratories took up its own block, apart from the rest of the factories. It was one of the few buildings that had siding. However, unlike most buildings, this siding appeared to be made out of bright white marble, until you looked closely enough and realized it was plastic.

Strange. I wasn't sure what the significance of the plastic was, unless it was just to make the building stand out, different (better?) than the rest.

In addition, the building was inset slightly from the sidewalk. Many of the factory buildings crowded right up to the edge, and anyone carelessly walking along would bump into the walls. Homonym Laboratories had a tall iron fence running around the property. The walls of the building didn't start for a few feet inside.

Fake grass ran between the fence and the wall. Was that a place where scientists would walk, trying to clear their heads after spending hours with complicated formulas?

A tall guard stood at the single gate that led through the fence. I did a double, then triple take.

That wasn't a Human guard. No, that was an actual warrior from Mars. He wasn't dressed in his traditional costume, which was merely a pair of pants, heavy boots, and a sleeveless cloak that left his muscular chest bare. Instead, he wore a guard's uniform, completely covered up in a black jumpsuit with a yellow badge sewn into the left shoulder. The only things that gave him away were his haircut—his straight brown hair flowed down to his shoulders instead of up off the collar like most men—as well as his flat, ape-like face.

It was almost impossible to get one of the warriors of Mars to do work such as guarding. It wasn't that they couldn't be hired. They just charged such an outrageous amount that no one could afford them for such menial work.

According to the rumors, warriors from Mars were impervious to bribes. That was one of the reasons why they insisted on being paid so much, so that there would never be any temptation for them to soil their honor or their word.

No wonder Pete had not been worried about the lab's security! There was no way I could ever manage to sweet talk my way into that fortress. It may as well have been located on Earth.

I still walked around the entire block, examining the building as I went. That was when I discovered that additional guards patrolled the greenway between the fence and the building, not eggheads.

If this were Earth, probably there would have been a dog or two as well.

Blinds hid everything going on inside the building. I was surprised that they even had windows.

One of the curious things I found as I circled the building was that there was a bridge, up on the third floor, that connected the first building to the building across the street. The bridge was completely covered, no windows, so you couldn't see anyone who used it.

The building across the street was probably the chemical factory, given the faint acidic scent wafting from it. Its door was on the far side, opposite the side of the building with the bridge, and though it only had regular guards, I figured it was just as unassailable.

I only passed by the front of the labs with the Mars warrior once more. He'd already pegged me as someone who didn't belong in the area. I knew that if he saw me circling the building a third time he might call the cops down on my head.

And I really didn't need any sort of entanglement with law enforcement at this point. Particularly not given the cachet that Homonym Laboratories seemed to carry.

I headed back to the train station, stymied. I couldn't get into that laboratory. Couldn't surprise Pete by just stopping by his office.

I went back into the city, tracing the other routes I knew Pete took on a regular basis. Went by the grocery store, picked up an apple for my breakfast. Went to the little café where he got his coffee and flirted with the waitress some before I settled in with my paper.

I kept an eye on the people who walked past, but I didn't catch a glimpse of anyone who looked like Pete.

His imposter seemed to be hiding from me.

Pete, at least according to the schedule he'd laid out for me, wouldn't leave his lab until three PM that afternoon. He always made a point of leaving early on Saturdays, only taking Sundays completely off, generally spending those days with friends.

I went back to my own apartment and napped, setting an alarm to make sure that I got up in time to be out at the train station when Pete got off.

I did not feel like a fifteen-year-old girl waiting breathlessly for her boyfriend. This was a client. I wanted to see him in his native environment.

I still put on a clean suit, combed my hair, and made sure my breath didn't stink.

I called myself all kinds of fool when I found myself wishing for a better mirror than the one on the bathroom medicine chest.

Still couldn't help but hurry out the door when the time came for me to see Pete again.

AS I WAS EARLY, I RISKED TAKING THE TRAIN OUT TO the factory district again. I was lucky and got there just in time to see Pete walking toward the station. He seemed preoccupied, staring at the ground and shaking his head as he walked, as if he was still trying to figure out some vital clue to the Universe.

There were only a few other men making their way to the station at the time, so I had the opportunity to watch him without being noticed.

Something was different about him that afternoon. Had his day gone so poorly? He seemed less confident than when I'd first seen him.

Before I could stop myself, I walked right up to him. "Hello, Pete," I said.

He startled, looking up. "Hello, Alvin and not Al," he said with that bemused smile of his.

Huh.

Either the effect of his looks faded rapidly or he really wasn't feeling like himself that afternoon. The eyes were still that intense green, his black hair perfect, lips full and sensuous.

But I was no longer attracted to him. In fact, the cynic in me was now yammering in my ear about what had actually happened the first time we'd met.

Had it been some sort of perfume that he'd been wearing? A hidden mind control ray?

Or was it just that familiarity bred contempt?

"I should have known that you'd be able to follow me here," Pete said. "Tell me, did you risk the laboratory security?"

"Even I know better than to try to mess with a warrior from Mars," I told him honestly.

He grinned and nodded, saying, "Good. I'm happy to know that the imposter can't just waltz in there and try to ruin my life with my bosses as well."

We fell into step and started walking toward the train station again. "Why do you suppose it is that the imposter started, well, impersonating you?" I asked. It was one of the questions that puzzled me the most. Was it because Pete, at least at first appearance, was so perfect?

Pete shrugged. "My nearly empty bank account might be part of the reason," he said. "I've instructed the bank manager that he must call me and actually speak with me before any more large withdrawals are made. We've set up a code. That way, if the imposter tries again, I can at least stymie him."

"Smart," I said. Though I was no longer as attracted to Pete, I could still see where that attraction had been. It left me with a sense of melancholy, not anger. "But why else? Since he can't break into your labs and steal all your secrets?"

Pete looked worried at that. "I sometimes have meetings with other scientists at company headquarters, downtown. There's a big one coming up Monday night. You don't suppose the imposter has plans to impersonate me there?"

"That sounds like an excellent time to take your place," I

said. "Particularly if there's delicate work that you'd be talking about."

We both entered the train before Pete responded. "It wouldn't be that difficult to gain access to the meeting. What, do you think the imposter would knock me out or something? In order to steal my place?"

"Possibly," I said. I explained my reasoning to Pete, how the bank hadn't really been a test of Pete 2's powers, how going to the grocery store, meeting people he saw frequently, was a much more accurate test. If he could trick those people into believing he was the original, he could probably fool the other scientists.

Pete gave me a huge smile for having figured all that out. "I think you're right," he said. "Particularly since I'm not speaking at this meeting, but just attending. While some of the other scientists only talk about science, there's a contingent that frequently argues politics and other such things. If he knows which scientists to speak with, even his own lack of scientific knowledge wouldn't trip him up."

"Interesting," I said. I had assumed that eggheads only talked "egg" as it were to their fellows. It was good to know that I might even have a chance to fit in at such an engagement.

We rode for a while in silence before I finally turned to Pete and said, "I think I have a plan. But it's going to take some coordination."

Pete nodded slowly. "Anything to catch this imposter before he does anything more to ruin my life."

"Then here's what we're going to do…"

PETE AND I SPENT THE REST OF THE WEEKEND together, as well as all day Monday.

No, not like that.

I didn't let him out of my sight once, though. I didn't want there to be a chance for the imposter to attack him, knock him out before Monday's meeting.

Though we ended up at Pete's much larger apartment, it still managed to drive me absolutely crazy to be in another person's space for so long. I had never thought of myself as a loner, just as someone who naturally spent a lot of time alone.

It was enlightening how much I craved being on my own again, how much I was looking forward to my solitary room.

Food for thought.

Pete turned out to be a pretty decent guy, particularly later that evening when I managed to get a couple of beers into him and he started talking. He was as intelligent as he looked, but not in just a scientist's manner. We could talk sports, politics, hell, he was even interested in some of my work and my cases.

I slept on the sofa while he crashed in his bed. We took turns showering and shaving, then I made him my special egg scramble for breakfast.

Though I rarely cooked, it was nice to be able to show off a little, to display that I did know my way around the kitchen. I didn't tell him why, of course.

When you have a mother who comes home at night from her secretary job and drugs herself out on pain killers, you learn at a young age how to fend for yourself.

I was still more relieved than I'd like to admit when the time finally came for us to go to the symposium. We didn't go together. Instead, I followed him, making sure that nothing hinky happened to him.

I liked Pete. I genuinely did. Every once in a while that old stirring of attraction reared its ugly head, but I managed to beat it back every time.

We took the train downtown, to one of the swankier hotels that was catering the event. The doorman wore a traditional double-breasted gray coat that went to his knees, along with white gloves and hat. Poor guy must be naked underneath to work in such heavy clothing. The brass doors led to an open reception area, with marble floors and enough touches of brass and dark faux wood to lend it an air of elegance. Quiet conversations filled the air that retained the faint scent of serious credits. None of this *nouveau riche* glitz, but old families with even older money.

Pete met me at the entrance to the Grand Ballroom, handing me a nametag that had been hastily made up with my name on it. That surprised me. I had assumed that he'd give me a false identity. Using my real name meant that others might recognize me.

Still, I smiled and clipped it to my good light-gray suit.

When we walked into the ballroom, I knew that I would be put immediately into my place. Some of the men and women here were obviously from the board of directors—you could tell by the fancy suits, dresses, and furs they wore. The rest of the men were probably scientists like Pete—lab rats with suits not much better than mine.

The conversations were low and muted. Not much laughter, more serious talk. It smelled of men's cologne and dry wool, the room temperature set a bit cooler by the staff so the room itself would be comfortable even with about a hundred bodies gathered.

There were cash bars in both back corners. Rafts of round tables set with fancy linens, crystal glassware and heavy silverware started about the middle of the room and marched toward the raised stage at the front. This was going to be a dinner and talking affair.

Pete and I both had a whiskey highball. It was too sweet, but the soda cut the taste of the cheap rotgut the hotel served. Then we wandered over to the group of eggheads who were the least likely to talk science at us. We ended up talking baseball, a thinking man's sport. Of course, they were far more into the statistics than I was, but it was still interesting.

I kept my eyes moving, watching the crowd, making sure that I didn't see Pete's imposter anywhere, say, dressed up as one of the hotel waiters making their rounds with the hors d'oeuvres—stale round pieces of hard bread with bland slices of tomato, cheese crackers that were dry and tasteless, and gummy potato puffballs. Now, I'm no gourmet, but even my bachelor skills could have produced something better.

Was probably going to have to pick up a sandwich on the way back to my apartment if these were any indication of what dinner was going to be like.

Finally, three women from the hotel staff walked in, ceremoniously carrying small xylophones made out of bright silver. They walked up to the first line of tables, then simultaneously began to play harmonized notes. It was a subtle but classic ringing of the dinner bell.

Given the lack of excellence of the food, it slotted the hotel into the right place for me.

All show, no substance.

Wasn't sure what that said about the company that had rented such a place.

The less said about dinner, the better. I continued to have bland conversations with men who didn't really have a clue how the real world worked, while eating mediocre food served on incredibly beautiful plates.

Just as dinner was ending, Pete excused himself. I had thought he'd be going to the men's room—but no, he walked up toward the front of the stage.

Seemed that Pete had underplayed his role that evening.

While he wasn't giving a talk, he did end up playing master of ceremonies for the other scientists.

Luckily, the wait staff was on hand with good, strong coffee, probably the best thing they served all night.

I watched Pete slide on and off the stage, introducing speakers, wondering why he hadn't bothered to tell me about what he was really doing.

The second time he came on stage, I saw the difference. This was the beautiful side of Pete. He sounded the same. Wore the exact same clothes. Had that same twinkle in his green eyes.

But I couldn't take my eyes off him. That attraction stirred, heavy in my belly.

The third time Pete came on stage, the attraction had worn its way thin again.

Before the end of the evening, I'd figured it all out. Not just Homonym Laboratories but this entire ruse, and who was actually the rat in the experiment.

I didn't bother waiting until the talks finished, just took myself back to my solitary apartment and my solitary life, certain for once what the morning would bring.

———

AS I'D EXPECTED, PETE SHOWED UP AT MY OFFICE EARLY the next morning. I was sitting behind my desk, my notes at hand.

However, not only did Pete walk in, but so did Pete 2, right behind him.

They were identical, of course. Natural born twins weren't as much alike. At least they wore different colored shirts under their matching suits, making it slightly easier to tell them apart—blue Pete and green Pete.

I didn't need the shirts. My Pete—the one I'd met first,

the one that still drew tendrils of attraction from me—was the one in the green.

"When did you figure it out?" my Pete asked.

"Friday afternoon, at the library," I said. "Literature about the company mentions making clones."

The two Petes looked at each other, surprised. What, I wasn't supposed to use that word? I was supposed to think that they'd been born that way?

Slowly, Blue Pete nodded, turning back to address me. "Which is the original?" he asked, curious, ever the scientist.

"You are," I told him. "Your clone has been 'perfected.'"

"Did we fool you for a while?" my Pete asked.

"Possibly. I knew there was something different about you," I said, pointing to Blue Pete, "when I met you outside the train station."

The two Petes looked at each other again. "I told you we tweaked the charm too much," Blue Pete said.

My Pete shrugged and smiled, first at his twin then at me. "But the charm is distracting, right?"

I gave him an appraising look. How much did I tell them? How much had they already guessed or plotted out in some mathematical formula? "Yes and no. It gave me a clue you were different," I said. "It also made me look harder at everything you said and did."

Blue Pete nodded. "We'll work on it."

"But why hire me?" I said. "Why come to me with this false story of impersonation?"

"We wanted to see if you'd ever be able to figure out the truth," my Pete said. "You have a good reputation. I wanted to see how long we could hoodwink you."

"So that you can hoodwink the public next?" I said, frowning.

"No, our intentions are good," Blue Pete assured me. "There's a shortage of women on the Moon, you know."

"Tell me about it," I said sourly.

"The figures Central posits are actually low," he continued. "But what if we could better those numbers?"

"Go on," I said, curious even though I knew better, knew that it was a con.

"We're still experimenting with creating doubles," my Pete said with a grin. "That process continues to be prohibitively expensive. And we've had no success in making women from men, or vice versa."

I kept my expression bland, though disappointment filled me.

No female version of Pete was coming down the line anytime soon.

"Each time we succeed, we work hard to make the clone the most perfect version of the original," Blue Pete continued. "Not just the girl of your dreams, but the perfect girl."

"And why would she consider a schmuck like me if she's so perfect? Why doesn't she go gallivanting off with someone just as perfect as her?" I asked reasonably.

Both Petes frowned at that. "We're working on it," Blue Pete said slowly.

"Sure you are," I said, not bothering to hide my scorn. "You're not working for people like me, but for your rich investors, the guys who could afford to have any girl they wanted in the first place." I shook my head. "You disgust me."

They nodded at the same time. It was kind of eerie how similar they were at that moment, just a single organism.

"Going to have to change the marketing plan," my Pete said after a few moments.

"You're already working on a 'more perfect you,'" I said. "Why stop there? A more perfect mate? A more perfect society?"

The two Petes stood up. They buttoned their jackets in the exact same manner, though my Pete was the only one who brushed at some piece of imaginary lint still sticking to the edge of his coat.

"No one likes being used," I scolded them, staying seated. "Particularly not the rat in his maze."

"But you were paid well. Rewarded handsomely, some might even say," Blue Pete said.

I shrugged. "Don't bother coming back."

My Pete raised an eyebrow at that, but then nodded.

I locked my office door after they'd gone. I told myself it was because I didn't want to see another poor mook's face that day, but it also might have been so I didn't go after them, to tell my Pete that I'd changed my mind and I'd like to see if we could become friends.

Or anything else.

For a long while after that case, I found myself watching the faces of the people who passed me in the street.

Were they the real original Loonie who'd immigrated to the Moon?

Or was that individual actually the more perfect version of themselves?

I wasn't likely to find out, not unless I got too damned close.

I was better off alone. Not just for now, but possibly, forever.

[4]

THE CASE OF THE BUNGLED BANK ROBBERY

HALLOWEEN ON THE MOON WAS ALWAYS SOMETHING, you know?

That year, the fancy store fronts on Main Street all had pumpkins in their displays. Not your ordinary Earth pumpkin, no, these were wearing fishbowl helmets—the kind you put on when you left the warrens and went for a stroll on the surface of the Moon. First one was clever. The rest should have come up with something different.

As for folks dressing up, there were the usual flocks of giggling girls done up in green makeup and white hair, supposedly imitating one of the natives from Venus. (They never had the right slink to their step, and none of them went the extra mile and wore dentures with sharp pointed teeth.) There were also the college boys who put on shirts with muscles painted on them, along with sleeveless long coats and monkey-like facemasks, pretending to be warriors from the caves of Mars. The best of those might have been threating to a kitten. Maybe.

I didn't do much decorating in my office—never got any kids coming my way, either for cases or looking for popcorn balls and candied necklaces. I'd hung up my shingle in the fishbowl warrens of Luna City. It had the advantage of being cheap. That was about it.

Besides, during Halloween or at any other time, the adults who came to see me weren't necessarily in the mood for fun and games.

I still taped a cut-out picture of one of the moon pumpkins onto the water cooler that burbled quietly in the corner. I figured that was festive enough. I left the black beat-up file cabinets in the other corner unadorned. I also didn't bother hanging anything from the slow fan in the middle of the ceiling that was more for show than to actually push around the stale air piped in by Central.

Halloween occurred on a Friday that year. I spent the night avoiding all the bars and the partiers, drinking by myself in my one-room bachelor apartment. Might have spent the entire weekend drinking, to be honest, not wanting to deal with the poor schmucks who thought that a little dress-up or make-believe was going to suddenly change their lives into a happy place.

Early Monday morning, I was back in my office nursing one hell of a hangover and swearing that I wasn't going to do it again.

I knew better, though. Halloween marked the start of the holiday season. Which meant my business was about to either get insanely busy as tempers started flaring or it would be as quiet as the dark side of the Moon.

I was writing up my notes from my latest case—mistaken identity between two men who, though they weren't related, were still close enough in appearance to be twins—when a loud knock on the door interrupted me.

"Come in!" I called, then I winced. Geez, I really shouldn't be raising my voice, not with this head of mine.

Whoever was at the door didn't hear me, as they just

knocked again, louder this time, rattling the frosted glass set in the door.

Normally, I would have just shouted. But instead, I got up from my comfortable chair, buttoned my suit jacket, then walked across the office to open the door.

The Human man who stood on the other side looked startled, as if he hadn't expected anyone to be in this early. He was short and pudgy, maybe five foot six. His bald head shone in the dim hallway light, though his eyebrows were black and bushy and a full mustache covered his upper lip. He had something of a tan which set him apart from the rest of us Moon rats. That meant he either had come from Earth recently or he was rich enough to take a nap on a tanning bed now and again.

He wore a white shirt with double stripes running down it, green in the center with golden edges. His brown suit, though rumpled, was made out of fine wool. A black tie hung loose around his neck.

"Can I help you?" I asked when he just stood there, mouth gaping.

"Are you Alvin? Alvin Goodfellow? PI to the stars?" he said, still flummoxed.

"That's what the jingle says," I said. Though the ads I ran on the radio claimed that I was the best PI on the Moon, Venus, or Mars, I really only had the one dinky office here on the Moon.

That just meant I got interesting cases, as well as the occasional rich mook like this guy.

"You have to help me!" he exclaimed. "I've been set up!"

"Why don't you come inside and tell me about it, Mr. ..." I said, reaching out with my hand.

"Bennett. Eugene Bennett," he said, automatically responding to the handshake, pressing his clammy palm against mine.

It was more like a flurry of movement than an actual handshake. He was trembling. I caught the odor of rank sweat. Was he frightened? I didn't trust that wild-eyed look he was giving me.

"Alvin," I said. "Alvin Goodfellow." I kept hold of his hand and dragged him inside the office, as he appeared to want to spill his guts on my doorstep.

"Oh! Oh. Thank you," he said, looking around nervously.

I shrugged and went back to my side of my desk, unbuttoning my suit jacket before I sat down. Though what I was wearing wasn't anywhere near as nice as his, I still had a reputation to retain as one of the good guys. I'd been born with a baby face—bright blue eyes, pale skin, and freckles scattered across my nose—as well as red hair that curled outrageously anytime I let it grow, even someplace as dry as the Moon.

I used all of that ruthlessly to put poor schmucks at ease. At least until it became more advantageous to knock some heads together.

Mr. Bennett sat down and took a few deep breaths, obviously trying to get himself back under control.

Whatever it was had worked him up good. I found myself hoping for an interesting case.

I should have known better than to ask for something *interesting*.

IT TOOK ME A WHILE TO GET MR. BENNETT SETTLED down, with a glass of water and a bit of small talk about how crazy the Halloween costumes had been that year.

Eventually, I was able to pull out a fresh notebook from my desk and say, "Tell me what happened."

He looked askance at the notepad. "Do you have to take notes?" he said.

"These are for my eyes only," I assured him. I waved toward the locked filing cabinets in the corner. "No one gets in those except me."

Though they were locked, anyone with enough enthusiasm and a strong paperclip could break into those cabinets. I wasn't about to tell him that.

He pressed his lips together, still worried.

I was happy to wait him out.

"All right, but you can't go to the papers or talk with anyone about this!" he insisted.

"I don't do this work for the publicity," I told him. It surprised me how much lower my tone got. He'd touched a sore spot I hadn't been aware of.

I really didn't do this job in order to be famous, no matter what my jingle might say. I loved the puzzle. The putting to rights. And yeah, the opportunity to sometimes knock heads together.

"All right," Mr. Bennett said, nodding. "I'm a manager at the Holdingbrook Mutual Provident bank."

I tried not to let my surprise show on my face. Holdingbrook was one of the privately held banks headquartered on the Moon. They only served the upper echelon of society. I wouldn't make enough in five years to warrant my shadow crossing their threshold.

Mr. Bennett didn't look nearly rich enough to be a manager there.

"You work with clients?" I asked.

Some of my disbelief must have seeped into my voice.

"Of course!" he blustered. When he saw me start to write that down, he quickly added, "Though mainly I manage the tellers."

That made more sense. He probably only ever saw the

rich clients crossing the fancy marble floor of the bank. He hadn't actually met or worked with any of them.

"As you know, the bank was robbed on Friday," Mr. Bennett continued. "They broke into the vault and took everything they could lay their hands on."

I didn't know, actually. Then again, I'd crawled into a bottle Friday night and hadn't bothered crawling back out again until Sunday.

I was going to have to buy a few newspapers and catch up on the news.

"The police think that it was an inside job," Mr. Bennett said. "And suspicion has fallen on me. Me!"

I had to admit that Mr. Bennett made a nice fall guy. He didn't appear as rich or as well connected as the bank managers who dealt with clients. It would be easy to place the blame on him.

"You have to help me, Mr. Goodfellow!" Mr. Bennett started shaking again. "I was at the police station all night being questioned. I came here right away after that. You must help me!"

That explained his rumpled suit and general appearance. Must have been quite an affront to his delicate system to be hauled off that way.

"Who are the detectives in charge of the case?" I said. Might as well get all of the bad news out of the way first.

"Detectives Evans and Schmidt," Mr. Bennett said. He reached inside his breast pocket and pulled out a business card.

Swell.

I glanced at the card then shoved it back at him. Evans wasn't too bad. Kind of a hard ass but also a stickler for doing things by the book. I knew him more by reputation than anything else.

Any cop with a good rep was hard to find. Particularly here on the Moon.

Schmidt, on the other hand, went out of his way to be an asshole. The pair of them played the "good cop, bad cop" routine all the time. However, even when Evans wasn't doing the good cop thing, Schmidt still played rough.

"Tell me the details of the bank robbery," I told Bennett.

"Surely you've read all about it," Mr. Bennett said stiffly. "That's all I've talked about now for over twelve hours."

"Just give me your impressions, then," I said. I really was going to have to get every newspaper I could lay my hands on to study up on this case.

"Halloween—it's always a mess, you know?" Mr. Bennett said. "I'd instructed the guards at the door to make sure no masks. Not that I was worried about a robbery," he assured me. "Our vault is one of the best on the Moon. Pressure sealed. Takes two keys to open it, plus the combination."

I nodded and smiled, hearing the propaganda for what it was. This was how the bank convinced their richest clients to leave their precious jewelry, art, and whatever else they valued in the vault. The bank, in turn, rented that security at a very pretty penny.

"Some of the costumes this year were just outrageous," Mr. Bennett opined. "Beyond the usual Venus girls and Mars warriors. There was one boy—it was quite clever, actually— who'd dressed himself up as that famous little boy blue painting. He carried a frame with him and everything."

"So when did the robbery occur?" I said, wanting to get my client back on track.

"Three-thirteen in the afternoon."

I raised my eyebrows at that. What, had he been looking at his watch or something?

"My girls, I mean, the tellers, always finish the last of their breaks at three-ten," Mr. Bennett said. "Though I think it's ridiculous that they have so many breaks during the day. They're there to work. Not to sit in the back room and gossip."

I didn't say anything. I was sure that "his girls" didn't last very long either, not if management had that sort of attitude. Then again, management usually had that sort of attitude when it came to the people who actually did the work.

"Normally, I sit at my desk, which is behind the counter, with the girls," Mr. Bennett said. "But one of my regulars had come in, and I'd gone out to speak with her. While I was there, I noted that Shirley was late coming back. Not by much, just a minute or so. I'd noted the time so that I could dock her if necessary. I needed to check my notes to see if it was her first infraction that month."

Yup. I wasn't looking forward to interviewing Mr. Bennett's girls, as they were sure to have a *lot* to say about their boss.

"Anyway, one of the other girls had just called me over—I think it was Mae, I honestly can't remember who it was—when I hear this meaty, male voice call out, 'Everyone put their hands in the air! Now!'" Mr. Bennett shuddered, the memory still overwhelming.

"When I looked over, I saw that it was a man—obviously a man—with a big beefy face and a five o'clock shadow, dressed up in a black-and-white nun's habit. He had the largest ray gun I've ever seen. He had to hold it with both hands," Mr. Bennett said, miming the action. "It had a long barrel out front, with many glowing rings circling it."

"Huh," was all I said. I'd seen such a ray gun before. That one had been mounted on an Army Jeep, and also on the dark side of the Moon. It could melt an entire mountain down to slag. I'd seen the demonstration as part of a different case.

Was it the same ray gun? Had it fallen into the wrong

hands? From the description of the nun, he might have been an Army grunt, big and beefy as most of them were.

"Two other men, also dressed like nuns, started shoving people to the floor. I was one of the first," Mr. Bennett said. He shivered. "I thought I was going to die. Of course I gave them my keys when they asked for them!"

"Did you actually have both keys to the vault?" I said, surprised. He wasn't high enough in the ranks to justify that, was he?

"Normally, no, I don't," Mr. Bennett said, flustered. "And that's why the police think I was in collusion with those other men. You see, we were short staffed that day. I was carrying Peterson's keys. He'd come down with some sort of intestinal issues. They sounded just awful." He wiped his hand over his mouth, then took a moment to smooth out his mustache.

Whatever Peterson had come down with must have been bad enough for Mr. Bennett to also consider vomiting.

"The robbers kept everyone down on the floor of the bank. I really do have to commend the cleaning crew, because from that vantage point, you can see every spec of dirt in the corners, and there wasn't any!"

That seemed like a very strange observation for a man supposedly in fear for his life.

"So the robbers split up? Some went to the vault and some stayed out front? What about your own guards?"

"I didn't learn this until later, but Sandy, the guy out front, had been overpowered by the nuns early. I mean, it wasn't my responsibility to manage security. That was Peterson's job. Evidently Sandy had been missing for close to an hour before the robbery took place." Mr. Bennett shook his head. "I didn't know to be worried! Not until it was too late!"

"What did the robbers take?" I said.

"They already had the combination, which again, means this was an inside job," Mr. Bennett assured me. "And since we were short-staffed, I had both of the keys. But I'm innocent! Really!"

I didn't believe him. No one was as innocent as he proclaimed. Maybe he hadn't hired the robbers, but he'd been involved in something hinky at the bank from the sound of his voice right now.

Was it part of this case? Maybe. Maybe not. I resolved to keep my eye on Mr. Bennett as well.

"What did they take?" I asked again.

"They took some things that were useless, like jewelry. They won't be able to sell that," Mr. Bennett said with confidence. "It's too easily identifiable."

I nearly rolled my eyes at his naivety. The robbers, if they were smart, would melt down the settings of everything they stole, then sell the jewels separate from the precious metals.

"But they also took all of the gold we had stored in the bank," Mr. Bennett finally confessed.

"Gold?" Why would a bank keep gold on the premises? We lived in a modern age. Sure, there were still coins and bills around, but a lot of businesses now operated strictly on credits.

"All our credits are backed by gold," Mr. Bennett said stiffly.

Now the gold made more sense. I knew some idiots had proposed devaluing the Luna credits so they weren't based on the gold standard. As I recall, the idiot got laughed out of Central and hasn't had a job since.

"It was the last day of the month," Mr. Bennett whined, wringing his hands.

God, that was an annoying habit. No wonder he was still lower management with no hope of promotion.

"We had our full reserve of gold ready to go off-world, to

the vaults in orbit," he said. "The robbers took everything. Everything!"

He seemed ready to weep over money that wasn't even his own. "The reputation of the bank is ruined," he added dramatically.

I shrugged. Sure, some of the rich boys might take their marbles and go play somewhere else. I was sure there were plenty of other suckers the bank could draw in. In the long run, Holdingbrook would be fine.

"I'm going to lose half my girls," Mr. Bennett said. "Oh, they haven't announced it yet. But I just know that will be one of the 'belt-tightening' measures that they take."

Of course, none of the managers would take a cut in pay. The annual holiday bonuses for the board wouldn't be savaged either. That would be asking far too much. No, just fewer actual workers to do the real work.

And Mr. Bennett would lose some of his prestige, such as it was, if he had fewer people reporting to him. Even if they were just girls.

"Can the police prove that you were working with the robbers?" I said. I figured that was all I was going to get out of Mr. Bennett at this point. The adrenaline was starting to wash out of him. He was growing paler.

"No! Of course not," came Mr. Bennett's automatic refusal. "It's all circumstantial. The fact that I had the keys. That I wasn't in my usual place behind the counter. That Sandy went missing and I didn't notice."

The last point was a little damning, but as for the rest, he had a point. The robbers had timed their heist perfectly, not only on the last day of the month but on Halloween as well, so they could take advantage of dressing up. No one would remember their faces, not really, not when they were wearing such outrageous costumes.

We negotiated my fees. I charged him double, as he looked as though he'd be good for it.

He didn't even blink an eye.

Was I going soft? Not charging enough anymore?

Or did this mook have more money than I'd thought?

He gave me his card and I told him I'd be in touch soon.

First, I had to go find some aspirin to get rid of the headache that was still banging away behind my eyes.

Then, I was going to have a talk with one of my connections.

Johnny the shoeshine boy usually worked the block kitty-corner to the bank. It was time to get some polish on my old black Oxfords. And more miles on the sole.

JOHNNY WAS IN HIS USUAL SPOT, ABOUT A QUARTER OF the way down the block from the Holdingbrook bank. He was easy to see, as he had a chair mounted firmly on a box, like a poor man's throne, where customers sat and he could more easily get at their shoes.

Holdingbrook wasn't on Main Street, but two blocks to the west, tucked in on a rich, quiet street.

All of Luna City was underground, of course. Though I'd heard talk of building great glass domes as part of Luna 2, I wouldn't be visiting there anytime soon. I'd grown up on the Moon, in the warrens. Not having a ceiling over my head unnerved me. Plus, I didn't care how good that glass was, how *unbreakable* it supposedly was either. I'd much rather be in a place where it was easy to close off a corridor in case of a breach. Dozens of lives lost, instead of hundreds or even thousands.

Most of the downtown buildings were two to three stories tall, carved out of solid moon stone. The fancier ones were then faced with polished rock or marble, some even with imported brick. The tall ceiling was lit with lights that overlapped, so it was easy to be fooled into thinking that it was a bright, sunny day, even though you never saw the sun.

The temperature was a regular seventy degrees. Central did their best to always keep the air clean and the heat stable, particularly in the nicer parts of the city.

That constant temperature also made it easier to see the division of society. The richest of the rich wore a lot of extra clothes—jackets, shawls, even raincoats—unnecessary clothing that the rest of us couldn't afford. I did wear a suit jacket, but most men at a certain level did. Women at that level tended to wear sweaters or light coats. It was the factory workers and other laborers who only wore what they needed to, shirts and pants and plain shoes.

Main Street held a lot of expensive department stores with huge window displays. The sidewalks and street were crowded with people doing their shopping, as well as gawking tourists.

The street where Holdingbrook was located was a lot quieter. Instead of giggling women with bags full of their shopping, there were serious men doing serious business. More than one bank was on this street, along with accountant firms and insurance companies.

Johnny did a brisk business here, all those men with money who needed to put on their best appearance for their clients. They couldn't appear too rich, as they didn't want to compete with their clients, but they still had to look a certain way for those people to trust them.

Most of the men on this street wore suits. Some even wore vests under their suit jackets.

I waited, standing across the street, while Johnny finished up with his current customer. I had my newspaper, which I read while leaning against the rough brick wall of yet another financial institute that wouldn't even let me in the door.

Mr. Bennett had told me most of the salient details of the robbery, about being short-handed so the robbers got everything they wanted. Mr. Peterson had been so sick his wife had called a doctor to the house to attend him.

Chances were, someone had poisoned Mr. Peterson. Damned near killed him if I was reading between the lines correctly.

I knew men who would fake their own horrible death in order to get away with something. Peterson probably wasn't that tough——chances were, he was another pudgy banker cut from the same cloth as Mr. Bennett.

Not innocent, but possibly not guilty of this crime.

As Johnny was finishing up, using a shining cloth on his current customer's wingtips, I strolled across the street to claim my spot as next in line.

Now, Johnny's skin was as black as they come, though the inside of his mouth as well as the palms of his hands were pink. He had a broad open face with a feckless smile that he used to his advantage, just as I used my own innocent appearance.

It was one of the things I admired about him.

He never wore a suit jacket. His white shirt had the sleeves rolled up above the elbows, showing his muscular forearms. He had on a stained leather apron to protect his shirt and his trousers. His own shoes were humble brown leather Oxfords, but they were always polished to a shine so sharp you could see your reflection in them.

"Yas, sir, there you go, sir," Johnny said as he finished off his latest client, a fat banker who sat and read the paper as if talking with someone like a shoeshine boy was far beneath him.

The man just grunted, dismounted from the chair and stalked away.

"Hey, boss," Johnny said indicating that the throne was now mine.

"Hey, Johnny," I said, handing him twice his usual fee.

That was another thing about Johnny that was smart. He always insisted on payment up front. Otherwise, I knew that idiots like the customer in front of me would stiff him.

Johnny looked over the bills then stuffed them into his apron pocket. The goofy grin disappeared and he got a sharp look in his eye. "Figure you want to know what I saw with the robbery, right?"

"You got the best eyes here, kid," I told him seriously.

I knew that some idiots believed that the color of Johnny's skin made him a lesser man. They were wrong. Just like the green color of the women from Venus didn't make them any less formidable.

Just different.

"It was after three—I know that because the deli over there had shut for the afternoon," Johnny said, pointing with his brush before he returned to rubbing the bristles in the round tin of polish.

I couldn't help but grin. That was a much more reasonable estimate than Mr. Bennett's "three-thirteen." The deep scent of the polish rose up, a dark earthy smell that reminded me of being a kid, building my own shoeshine box in shop.

"I didn't know what was happening at first," Johnny said as he started to coat my shoes in polish. Though the initial polish was a softer black than my Oxfords, he knew what he was doing. I trusted Johnny.

He was actually one of the very few people I could say that about.

"I did see the three nuns come out of the bank. They

carried large Army-like duffle bags, you know, the color of that grayish camouflage soldiers wear doing exercises out on the regolith," Johnny said.

I nodded. It didn't surprise me that Johnny knew terms like "regolith" and used them properly. And that he knew that the Army base on the dark side of the Moon had a darker camouflage system.

"I even joked with the guy I was working on at the time, something about how they must have just gotten all their candy early," Johnny added. He flashed me a quick grin, his teeth oh-so-white contrasting with that dark skin of his.

"The nuns split up right away. One went up the block, the other came this way, then cut up, and the third went right across the street and into the building there," Johnny said.

"What's in that building?" I asked.

"There's an insurance firm, and an accountant's office. But I'd swear that he didn't go through either of those doors, but into the one between them, which leads to an empty office, upstairs, above the street. It's possible I'm wrong. But I'd swear he went through the door in between the other offices."

"Did you tell the cops?" I said, curious.

"Heck no," Johnny said, glaring up at me. "Not that they would have asked someone like me."

I nodded. Evans might have listened if Johnny had come forward with any information. But Schmidt wouldn't have bothered. Might even have roughed Johnny up some, just for the fun of it, or because he thought he could get away with it.

Schmidt had no idea how close he was to the line that would get him shivved in a dark alley someday.

"Anything else?" I asked as Johnny finished off applying

the polish to the first shoe, letting it soak in, while he moved on to the second one.

"Nope. Not really. Cops came and closed off the street. Good thing I'd already moved my station down some from the corner. Got some real business that afternoon, people wanting to rent my chair just so they could see above the crowd," Johnny said, flashing me another smile.

"Good," I told him. "I hope you gouged them well." I didn't see anything wrong with making a good profit off other people's lollygagging.

"You bet I did," Johnny said. "Had some nice upstanding citizens commend me on my business sense." He rolled his eyes. Stupid bankers probably had been surprised that anyone other than themselves was capable of making a profit.

"There wasn't much going on after that. I closed up shop early, having made my credits for the day." He listed a number, just to see my eyebrows rise up.

Huh. He was making more per day than I was.

I supposed he earned it. He worked a lot harder than I did, and had to deal with more assholes to boot.

"How did you know that the nuns were actually men?" I said after a moment, going back over his story in my head.

"They stripped off their wimples as soon as they hit the street," Johnny said. "I figure by the time they got a block away, those habits of theirs would be stuffed into any convenient trashcan."

That made sense.

The robbers had planned their robbery down to the last detail, as well as their getaway. They might already be headed down to Earth with their gold.

"What about the gun?" I asked.

Johnny's eyebrows creased as he thought. Finally he looked back up at me. "What gun?"

"Supposedly they had a wickedly long ray gun that they were threatening people with," I said.

"Nope. Didn't see a gun," Johnny said. He'd finished with the first coat of polish, wiped that off, and was now applying the buffing cloth, bringing out the true shine of the leather.

Huh. None of the newspaper accounts had said that the ray gun was found in the bank. Yet, more than one eyewitness had talked of the very large gun the first nun was toting.

Something so big wouldn't fit under one of their habits. Where had the gun gotten to?

By the time Johnny finished shining my shoes, they looked brand new. Expensive even. He sure had a way with that brush of his.

"There ya go, boss," Johnny said, falling back into his patter again.

I nodded and grunted, playing my part as rich white man. I dismounted the throne and looked around, considering my options.

I couldn't just go into the bank and interview the tellers. I wasn't officially part of the investigation, and Mr. Bennett had been given the week off. Without pay, of course. I'd have to figure out another way to talk to his "girls".

In the meantime, I was going to check on the empty offices across the street from the bank.

I nodded my thanks to Johnny, who just grinned at me.

With my newly shined shoes, I had a lighter step. Possibly even a lighter heart.

Who knew? Maybe my luck had finally changed, and I was going to be able to solve this case quickly.

As Jonny had described, there were three doors directly across the street from the Holdingbrook bank. One led into an insurance agency that had a receptionist's desk stretched across the front of the entire office. A pretty young woman sat typing away. No one could have just waltzed in and gone out the back without being noticed.

The accountant's office was the same, though it was a dour looking man sitting at a desk going over his books.

The third door, in between those two, had the name "J. R. Erwin, Esq." scratched out. I tried the door—locked. I pressed my face against the cold glass. Just beyond the entrance stood a darkened staircase.

So the lawyer's office had been on the second floor. I stepped back and looked up. Yup. Good view of the street as well as the bank from up there. Anyone sitting up there could see everything going on down below.

I stepped back to the door, trying the handle again. Would there be any clues upstairs? I doubted it. This group of criminals seemed too organized to just leave evidence lying around. Still, I wanted to get up there to take a look for myself.

I rattled the door a third time. Probably wouldn't be too hard to pick the lock, except for all these upstanding citizens who would see me do it.

"Coming! I'm coming!" came a man's voice from up the street.

I turned to see who was calling. A man with a harried look came bustling up. Tall and slender, mid-thirties, with sandy blond hair already starting to silver. He had a large set of keys in his hand. "Sorry, detective!" he said as he rushed to the door. "I only just now got the call."

So, the police were coming to investigate the former law office. Probably Evans and Schmidt. That meant I didn't have a lot of time to look around. The precinct was a few blocks away, and they'd probably called as they were leaving.

"Thanks," I told the man as he hurriedly opened the door. "I'll only be a minute."

I strode past him and went quickly up the stairs. He didn't take the hint and followed me up.

At the top of the stairs, a hallway led around to the left, back toward the front of the building. A window there provided an excellent view of the street as well as the bank. The air smelled musty and held a slight chill. Closed doors lay on either side. The one to the left was metal painted black, with a large sign that said, "PRIVATE!" on it. I checked the handle—it was locked. It was above the insurance agency, and was possibly extended offices for that scam.

The door to the right looked like the door to my office, with frosted glass on the top half and the name "J. R. Erwin, Esq." in gold letters across it. That door was unlocked and I let myself in.

"That shouldn't be unlocked," I heard the man with the keys mutter behind me.

So maybe the robbers had left a clue.

The office was larger than I'd expected, maybe thirty feet long and twenty deep, with broad windows all along the front wall. Old desks, in much better shape than the banged up one I had in my office, were scattered across it. No chairs or filing cabinets. A fine coat of dust lay across every flat surface. No fingerprints, though. The criminals were too careful for that.

However, there appeared to be a bag under the third window. I walked over to it, the other man crowded in close enough to be my shadow.

"That shouldn't be there," he said.

I contained my sigh. Seemed as though I had my own Greek chorus.

The bag looked like the ones that Johnny had described, made out of gray canvas cloth that the Army used on the other side of the Moon.

I knelt down and unzipped it. I didn't understand what I was seeing at first. It looked be a jumble of colored rings from a child's game. There was a brown, "L" shaped piece at the bottom of the bag. Only when I pulled it out did I realize that it was also a child's toy—the broken off stock of a kid's ray gun.

This was actually the huge gun the nuns were carrying. It had been assembled out of children's toys. It had never been real, but no one had gotten a good enough look at it to realize that.

Strange, the nun's habit wasn't in the bag as well. I would have thought if they'd left the gun behind, they might have also left behind their costume.

Maybe they had a real nun somewhere that they had to return the habit to.

"That will be all," I told the man as I stood back up. I started heading for the door. I knew I didn't have a lot of time.

"Are you just going to leave that there?" the man asked, pointing at the bag.

"My colleagues will be by shortly to pick it up," I said, glancing back at him.

"Colleagues, eh?"

Crap.

Whatever luck I'd been riding that morning had just run out.

Detectives Evans and Schmidt stood in the doorway.

That headache of mine was suddenly a whole lot worse.

AT LEAST THE DETECTIVES PLAYED ALONG FOR A WHILE, telling the man with the keys that he could leave, that they'd call him when he should come back and lock up the building again.

I could tell he didn't like it, but he didn't complain too loudly.

He was far too much of an *upstanding citizen* to want to antagonize the cops.

"So what are you doing here?" Detective Evans said, easily falling into the good cop routine. He was a tall man, even for a Moon rat—six foot five, at least—with a long, hangdog face and a reddish, bulbous nose that was starting to show evidence of being stuck in a bottle too often. He wore a cheap brown suit and a wide tie. His jacket didn't fit that well, and his hands hung out far beyond the sleeves, the knuckles bruised.

Had he actually been playing the part of the muscle for once? Not just letting Schmidt do all the dirty work?

Schmidt, on the other hand, was short, round, and more nattily dressed. His navy-blue suit was double breasted and had a subtle white pinstripe to it, while his black-and-white wingtips were the latest style. Beady dark eyes peered out from his pudgy cheeks. His small mouth had a natural sneer. Probably no one but his mother had ever thought he was innocent of anything.

"Got a tip that something hinky was going on here as part of the bank robbery," I told them straight up. "Come check this out."

Schmidt sauntered forward, as if he didn't have a care in the world, while his partner stayed by the door. He squatted down next to the bag and peered inside. "Kid's toys?" he asked in disbelief.

"Appears to be," I told him. Then I clued Evans in. "Big gun wasn't real. Just a bunch of rings put together to look like a huge ray gun."

Evans looked as though he wanted to spit in disgust. "Swell," he said. "And what little birdy told you about that?"

"No one, officer," I said innocently.

Schmidt stood up abruptly.

"No, really," I said, hands up, taking a step back. "I discovered this up here, same as you."

"How did you know that the robbers had been using this empty office to case the bank?" Evans asked, still sounding like he was merely a concerned citizen.

"It's obvious, right? All you had to do was walk past the bank and look across the street to see the office wasn't currently occupied," I said.

Schmidt shook his head. "I know guys like you don't work for free. Who's your client? Who are you protecting?"

"I'm not protecting anyone," I said. "As for my client, that's none of your business." I did have a reputation to uphold as one of the good guys. I didn't brag about my clients, not even in my ads. "I'm just trying to make sure justice is served."

"'Cause you're all about justice, right?" Schmidt asked, rolling his eyes.

I just shrugged. I actually was, more or less.

"Should we run him in for breaking and entering?" Schmidt looked over his shoulder at his partner.

Evans gave a mirthless smile. "Could take him in for impersonating a police officer. I'm sure the real estate agent would be happy to corroborate."

Swell. Now Evans was going to give me a hard time? What did I have to give them, that wouldn't give Mr. Bennett up?

"You know who my next call was going to be?" I said,

stalling for time as Schmidt started to unbutton his suit jacket, getting ready to "subdue" me before bringing me in.

"Who?" Evans said, staying where he was.

"Colonel Leavenworth," I said. "I've seen a gun like this one when I was working with him. Not many people knew it existed. Where do you think the robbers got the idea from?"

Schmidt stopped unbuttoning his jacket and looked back over his shoulder at Evans, who was peering at me with narrowed eyes. Then he gave a sharp nod and turned and walked out the door.

Moving faster than I'd anticipated, Schmidt turned back and gave me a solid punch in my gut. I doubled over, breathing hard.

"That's just a reminder to stay out of police business," he snarled. He rebuttoned his jacket, picked up the bag, and headed out the door.

I stayed where I was, doubled over, breathing through my nose so I didn't end up spewing the toast and coffee I'd had for breakfast all over the floor.

I knew I'd gotten off easy. Schmidt could have taken his time pounding me for no other reason than because the brass at the precinct were riding his ass about solving such a high-profile crime quickly.

What they didn't know was that I actually hadn't been about to call the colonel. We hadn't parted on the best of terms. Embezzlement cases sometimes went that way, particularly when more than one set of sticky fingers were in the pot.

I stayed where I was, up in the office, looking out on the street. Schmidt's punch had packed a lot of wallop. Later that night I was sure I'd find a fist-shaped bruise in the center of my stomach. Funny enough, the pain in my gut sure made my headache disappear. Seemed that focusing on breathing and forcing myself to stand upright chased away hangovers.

Not a cure I wanted to try again.

Nobody bothered me up in that office. I assumed that the nice detectives wouldn't bother calling the real estate agent about locking the door until they got back to the precinct.

I spent some time slowly stumbling between the desks, seeing if there was anything else left behind by the crooks. Didn't find anything, though.

The office was a nice enough joint. Wouldn't mind having a spot like this someday.

Then again, I probably wouldn't get the interesting cases if I had a high-figure office. And this many desks meant staff. People I'd have to deal with every day.

Didn't think any job would pay enough to be worth that.

I went back to the window to watch the rich, important people entering and leaving the bank. Holdingbrook appeared to be doing a brisk business today. All the managers would be working overtime, reassuring their richest clients that the bank was still secure, as were their personal belongings.

A young woman left the bank and hurried down the stairs. Instead of a fur coat or an impressive cloak, she wore merely a red cardigan over a plain gray skirt, with stockings and sensible shoes. Her dark wavy hair was pinned back and her face was scrubbed clean and honest.

I was heading for the door before I even realized I was moving.

That girl was probably one of the tellers. I was just going to have to suck it up and ignore my pain so I could go and talk with her.

The worst she could do would be to slap my face for my impertinence.

Wouldn't be the first time something like that had happened. Nor the last.

"Excuse me. Excuse me! Miss. Miss!" I said as I jogged along, one hand holding my gut. Geez, she was tearing a streak down the sidewalk. Where was she going in such a hurry?

Finally, she seemed to catch a clue that someone was calling her and looked over her shoulder. She frowned at me —what appeared to be the natural state of her otherwise pretty face. She had broad hazel eyes that had a shrewishness I didn't trust. She was wearing a touch of lipstick, but that was it. Just enough to make a girl feel pretty, or so I'd been told.

"Are you one of the tellers at Holdingbrook Mutual Provident?" I asked.

"We're not supposed to talk to reporters," she said primly.

"I'm not a reporter, ma'am," I said, handing her one of my business cards. "I'm a detective."

She looked at the name, then looked skeptically at me. "I've heard of you," she said. "You don't look like much of a detective."

"Looks can be deceiving," I told her with a broad wink. "Like you, for example. Hard working girl like you whose brilliance has been overlooked. Am I right?"

She nodded slowly.

"No one gives you the credit you deserve," I said, sidling next to her, trying to gain her confidence.

She rolled her eyes at me. "Tell me about it! I should have had that promotion to head teller. Not that old hag Mrs. Larson."

I nodded in sympathy. "Anyone could tell that you're the smart one, Shirley, right?" I had glanced at her name under the cardigan. I'd only caught the first letter, but hopefully, I was guessing right.

"That's right," she said. Then she sighed. "Look, I'd like to talk with you and all but I've got to get to the chemist's shop. My mom's still complaining about her toothache and needs more pain killer."

That sent a shudder down my spine but I kept a bland smile pasted to my face. "Is that why you were late last week? Because you were getting something for your mom?"

"How did you know? I guess you *are* a good detective," she said, nodding. "Mr. Bennett was going to dock me for being two minutes late. Two minutes! When he doesn't ever stop the other girls from gossiping all the time. They rarely do all the work I do." She sounded peeved.

"How about this? I'll go and get the powders for your mom, so you won't be late returning from your break this time," I told her. "That way, you can talk to me a little."

"Would you do that for me? That would be swell," she said.

Poor kid was just looking for someone to believe in her. "Course I would. It's in my name. Goodfellow," I said, repeating the commercial jingle.

She smiled at me. It looked strained, as if she wasn't used to making that motion with her face.

"So tell me what happened Friday afternoon," I said. "Don't worry," I assured her when she immediately got a worried look on her face. "Anything you say to me is strictly confidential. You can be my confidential source. No one will ever know it came from you."

"Thanks," Shirley said. "I really can't afford to lose this job. Not with my mom being sick all the time."

I nodded and swallowed against a dry throat. I'd been there, too. Trying to provide for a sick mother. Then it had turned out that it wasn't her being sick at all, but those damned pills the doctors kept prescribing for her.

"Was there anything unusual that you noticed when you came back in from your break?" I said.

She shook her head. "No. And the police asked that same question," she added accusingly.

"Was there anything good you remember from that time? Or something bad?"

That got her thinking along a different path. "There was something good. Mr. Bennett wasn't at his desk to harangue me when I came in late. He was out on the bank floor."

"Was that unusual?" I said. I'd wondered about that.

She shrugged. "He didn't do it all the time, but it wasn't unusual. He'd try to go out and sweet talk some of the little old ladies when he saw them come into the bank." She gave a very unladylike snort. "As if they'd ever give him the time of day. They know he's a gold digger, already on the lookout for his next victim."

"What do you mean?" I said. I hadn't had any time to investigate my newest client, though I'd meant to.

"He married rich," Shirley said. She lowered her voice, in order to share the gossip. "The only reason he has a job at Holdingbrook is because of his wife."

Mr. Bennett couldn't have married that rich since he still had a job, and it wasn't that high of a position. "You said he's looking for his next victim," I said, trying to build up a better picture of him.

"Mrs. Bennett has taken to her bed, or so I've heard," Shirley said, leaning in closer.

I got a whiff of her lily-of-the-valley perfume. Made me suddenly wish for things I couldn't afford. Not now, at least.

"Mr. Bennett has been frantic with worry," Shirley continued. "Once Mrs. Bennett is gone, he's gone, if you know what I mean. The board won't have him around anymore."

"But wouldn't he inherit everything?" I asked.

"There's not much left to inherit. Seems Mr. Bennett has a problem with the ponies."

That surprised me. Betting on horses was a tricky business, because the races were all held down on Earth. Took too long for the race results to be broadcast up here. Most people realized it was a sucker bet.

"Or maybe he was betting on the rats," she said in a snide tone.

I snorted. I didn't think that Mr. Bennett would stoop so low. I was actually surprised that a nice girl like Shirley was aware of the "rat races" as it were.

Groups of poor, desperate individuals would grow rats to huge sizes, as big as cats, then put them into a ring together to watch them tear each other apart. Whichever poor animal survived was declared the winner. Didn't see much sport in it at all, quite frankly.

"Whatever it was, he's already spent almost all her money," Shirley said. "When she dies, there won't be anything left."

"I see," I said.

Was Mr. Bennett actually desperate enough for money that he'd collude with bank robbers? But why then should he hire me?

"Look, the chemist's shop is just down the street," Shirley said. She pulled a script from her purse. "If you can just get this filled, that would be swell."

"Of course," I said, giving her my winningest smile. We arranged to talk again later that evening, after she'd finished work at the bank.

I didn't want to fill this quack's prescription. I knew what it was. It was what had started my mother down her path to addiction. These sorts of pills were exactly why she was in a home now and barely recognized me even on the good days.

I'd promised Shirley that I would pick up these pills. I had to think of something else though.

Some promises were meant to be broken.

_____

I KEPT THE MEETING WITH SHIRLEY LATER THAT NIGHT, though I kept it short. Not only did I not want to give her any ideas, I didn't want my own treacherous libido to get involved. Particularly not when it became obvious that Shirley had not only reapplied her lipstick, she'd also used more of that lovely perfume.

We met at the Blue Note Café. I'd chosen it because it was already closed by the time she got there.

"Do you want to go someplace else?" Shirley asked as she came up and saw me standing outside.

"I've got another clue I need to chase down," I said, lying with a really nice smile.

"Oh. All right," she said, though she sounded disappointed.

"But I got the pills you asked for," I said, handing her a thick sheet of paper folded sharply around two dozen white tablets.

She gave me a suspicious look. "These aren't the same as what I've been getting," she said. "These are white. Not pink. Are you sure these are right?"

"My mom was sick a lot, and in pain, too," I told her. "These were the best ones she ever took. However, instead of just swallowing them, your mom needs to suck on them for a bit first. That way, the medicine will work through her whole body."

"Really? Wow. Thank you," Shirley said as she put the

packet with the pills into her purse. She sighed. "I worry about my mom, you know? She's sick so much. And constantly in pain."

I nodded. Really. I'd been there. Which was why I'd given her sugar pills, coated with an analgesic. They would cause her mom's mouth to go a little numb as she sucked on them, but they wouldn't actually be bad for her. She couldn't get addicted to them.

They'd worked for a while with my mom, too. She kept saying she was getting better on those pills.

Then she went to see a different quack and got hooked again.

Shirley and I were both quiet for a moment.

"Thank you again," I told her. "You were really helpful." And she had been. That night, I was planning on doing some detective work.

I'd be tailing Mr. Bennett, my client.

"Sure. Anytime," Shirley said.

"So. Good night," I said. I nodded to her sharply.

I did *not* need to walk her to the train station. I was sure she'd be fine on her own. It wasn't as if we were in a bad neighborhood.

"Good night," Shirley said with a sigh.

We each went our separate ways. I felt bad about crushing whatever fantasies she may have been nursing about maybe dating a famous detective.

I couldn't afford such things. Not even as daydreams.

MR. BENNETT LIVED IN A NICE QUIET NEIGHBORHOOD, west of the downtown area. Most of the residents of Luna City lived in tiny apartments. Space was at a premium because it all had to be dug out of the ground. We weren't on the surface, at least not yet.

The block where the neighborhoods changed was obvious. Instead of buildings with just one door and lots of windows where the flats were, it was one long building with several doors. Townhouses, all connected, and two stories tall. I didn't know if those would be better than an apartment building or not. They looked narrow, and you had stairs you'd be going up and down constantly. At least you wouldn't have neighbors up above you.

A few blocks further west were actual individual houses for the richest of the rich. I'd read in a magazine how some of those houses even had skylights built into their roofs that opened up onto the surface of the Moon. I don't think I'd ever trust the technology of glass that way. I'd much rather have solid rock over my head.

Mr. and Mrs. Bennett lived in the center of one such rowhouse. It looked like a nice enough place, completely indistinguishable from its neighbors. There was no yard out front, of course, no stoop where people might gather and chat. Wouldn't surprise me, though, if there were a neighborhood community center nearby, a closed club that only people from this area could use.

The problem with such a sparsely populated neighborhood, particularly later in the evening, was that there really wasn't any place to do surveillance from. Central never turned off the lights in places like this, just dimmed them some to imitate night. There weren't any cars in the street. I did pass by a few electric bicycles. I walked past the Bennetts' house, then around the corner.

A small bodega, still open, was midway up the block. Maybe I'd have to stop there for a cup of coffee or something when I walked by again.

I squared the block, walking by lots more townhouses,

before heading back to the Bennetts'. It reminded me of the quads that made up Luna U—all the buildings around the edges of the block, while the center was possibly an open area, privately shared by all the residents.

On the second pass by the Bennetts' house, I slowed down. Mr. Bennett appeared to be leaving the house. Interesting.

Was he on his way to the bodega to pick up something for the wife? Had he gone stir-crazy from being cooped up all day? Or was he on some other mission?

I gave him a block head start before I turned around and started following him.

Hopefully, he was going to go someplace interesting.

I KEPT TRYING TO GUESS WHERE MR. BENNETT WAS going. He wasn't going to the bank, or to downtown. I caught the same train as he did, though I rode a different car and nearly missed him when he got off.

It finally occurred to me that Mr. Bennett was on his way to *my* office, in the fishbowl warrens. He wasn't dressed appropriately at all in his fancy suit and stuck out like cracked glass on a helmet—not enough to get you killed, but more than enough to make everyone around you really uneasy.

During the "daylight" hours that Central kept, there were a lot more people in the hallways and corridors, plus streams of factory workers when shifts changed. As there were other offices near mine, someone like Mr. Bennett wouldn't be as conspicuous.

As it was, even with the lights dimmed to "night-time," Mr. Bennett kept getting strange looks.

And more covetous looks than I felt comfortable with.

I finally walked up to him just as he was entering the building that held my office.

"Ah, there you are," Mr. Bennett said. "I was wondering when you were going to catch up."

That surprised me. Had Mr. Bennett known I was tailing him the entire time?

"I saw you walking past my house, you know," he said slyly.

"I'll have to be more careful next time," I said, stung. I'd known there wasn't a good place to do surveillance from his neighborhood. I should have been more clever, come disguised or something.

Not as a nun, but maybe as a delivery boy. Next time.

"I was very happy to see you," Mr. Bennett announced as I unlocked the door to my office and turned on the light.

The chairs were in the exact same place that I'd left them. A silver thread was still stuck to the back of one of them, so no one had been in while I'd been gone.

"Please, sit," I told him, offering him water again, though this time he refused.

"Anyway, I remember something that the robbers said, that I hadn't remembered before," Mr. Bennett said. He kept his hands neatly folded as he leaned on my desk.

Strange. Where had this self-possessed man been the first time he came to my office?

"The two went into the back, to the vault, and they left just the one out front. After they'd taken all the gold, when the two came back out, they said something like, 'Meet at the red track.' Does that mean anything to you?" Mr. Bennett continued to play it cool, as if he were discussing a meeting of the board of the bank, not a group of powerful, frightening crooks.

"It does," I said thoughtfully. I knew exactly where they'd be going, what part of the warehouse district on the east side of the city that they'd be in. It didn't surprise me that someone like Mr. Bennett had no idea where that was. I'd only recently learned about it myself, as part of a different case.

"Did you tell the police what you've remembered?" I asked pointedly.

"No, of course not," Mr. Bennett said. He seemed to recall his role as victim, and he shook his head hard. "They still think I'm 'in on it,' as it were."

I couldn't help but grimace. That sounded like Schmidt, all right.

"So. Are you going to go stop them?" Mr. Bennett asked, expectant.

"These were big, burly, Army men, right?" I said, remembering the description Mr. Bennett had given, as well as in every account I'd read.

"Yes," Mr. Bennett said. "They called the one with the large ray gun 'Sarge.'"

I raised my eyebrows but didn't say anything. No one else, at least according to the newspapers, had recalled that name being used.

"So, the red track is out in the warehouse district," I said.

Mr. Bennett's eyes grew wide as he thought through the implications of that.

"I'm not sure I want to go all the way out there, at night, by myself, to confront three robbers who are probably all more muscled than I am," I pointed out.

"Oh, you won't be alone. I'll go with you," Mr. Bennett said helpfully.

"Unless you have a lot more training than I do, I'm not sure that's a good idea," I told him.

"Well, we'll be armed, of course," Mr. Bennett said.

Normally, I don't go out with my ray gun. I generally

kept it tucked away in my desk. I tried to be smart, and to not put myself into situations when I needed to use it.

"Do you have a gun?" I asked, my regrets about taking this case starting to build.

It was going to mean a lot of work and I was pretty sure at this point that I wasn't going to get paid.

"Yes," Mr. Bennett said. He pulled what I would have called a lady's ray gun out of his jacket pocket. Had it at one time been his wife's gun? It had sleek lines and a mauve barrel, with a white diamond pattern along the back of the handle. It was easy to hide in the palm of your hand, compact and lightweight. It also packed one hell of a punch. A single tickle of this gun would stun a man twice my size, knock him out for twenty minutes or more.

It was also easy to modify to be much more powerful. I would bet that this one had been already. Just narrow the beam and it could become deadly.

Fortunately, the model was compatible with my own.

"Can I see that?" I said, keeping my tone as well as my face casual.

Mr. Bennett hesitated.

Unless he agreed, I was walking away from this case, though he didn't know that.

"I think you've got some problems with the charge," I lied smoothly.

Mr. Bennett looked at the gun, looked at me, then reluctantly handed it over.

"Now, you see here?" I said, showing him the barrel and pointing to one of the diamond decorations. "You're nearly out of charge." I shook my head at him and pulled out my own larger ray gun. "See?" I pointed to the green bar on mine. "You need a new battery. You're in luck that I happen to have one."

I swapped out batteries for him and handed his gun back

to him. He accepted it and slipped it into his pocket without really looking at it.

So far, so good.

"There are a few warehouses out on the red track that we could check," I said musingly. "Any idea which one they'd be in? Did they mention a number?"

Mr. Bennett shook his head morosely. "No. None at all."

"Then we'll just have to go and see if there's activity at any of them," I said. I tucked my own ray gun into the waistband of my pants, then stood up, buttoning my jacket over it.

Unless you were looking, you probably wouldn't even notice the bulge.

"Let's go get them," I said with my winning smile. "It'll be nice to show the police up one more time," I added with a chuckle.

Mr. Bennett seemed to believe me. "That would put another feather in your cap, wouldn't it?" he said with a condescending smile.

I merely nodded and led the way out of the office.

There was something rotten with this entire setup.

I just hoped that some sort of luck had come back my way, or this would end up being a very long night indeed.

———

I ASKED MR. BENNETT ABOUT HIS WIFE AS WE TRAVELED by train to the far side of the city.

"You've been checking up on me," he said coolly. "I did see you talking with Shirley, though." The way he pressed his lips together made me slightly worried about her. "Yes, my dear Tabatha is sick and has taken to her bed. But the doctor thinks that the new pills he's prescribed for her are going to do the trick this time."

"Was it nice to be home and able to take care of her all day?" I asked pointedly.

He gave me a reassuring smile. "Oh, what I wouldn't do in order to be with her all the time!" he proclaimed. "She's my angel, you know," he confided. "I don't know what I'd do without her. I'd be so lost."

I didn't believe a word of it. "It must be so nice," I said. "I'm still a bachelor. Married to the job."

"Ah, as much as I love my Tabatha, I will admit that I envy you your freedom. Able to come and go as you please with no responsibilities," Mr. Bennett said with a faraway look in his eye.

I had responsibilities, more than he realized. I had to work my ass off to keep a roof over my head, as well as make enough to afford the office and the ads. Plus, I paid for that fancy home my mother stayed in and all the medication she needed. I ate my meals alone in my one-room apartment, generally over the sink. I drank alone, sometimes too much. My best friend was probably the bartender down the street, and I only saw him when I felt flush and he was working.

It was just my imagination that I caught a whiff of that lovely lily-of-the-valley perfume that Shirley had been wearing.

Yet another thing that I didn't have.

When Mr. Bennett looked expectantly in my direction, I just shrugged at him. "We all have our own crosses to bear," I said lightly.

"That we do," Mr. Bennett said. "Tell me, are you a religious man?"

I shrugged. "I'm not a papist, if that's what you're asking. Shocked by men in nun's habits." I knew that some of the newspapers had been using that angle in their reports, how disturbing it must be for rough men to take something so sacred for such a sacrilegious act. "I don't make it to church often." Mom had dragged me there when I was young, though generally that had only been for Easter and Christmas.

"I'm not a religious man either," Mr. Bennett said. "I believe that good things come to those who do right by the world, though."

"Will you be deserving of such things?" I asked, curious how Mr. Bennett saw himself.

"Yes," he said fervently. "God helps those who help themselves."

That phrase wasn't actually in the bible. I wasn't about to point that out to him. I was sure that Mr. Bennett had helped himself to a lot, and often.

Just how much more he was going to reach out and take would be answered by the end of the evening.

There were at least half a dozen warehouses on the red track, which was located on the far eastern side of all the warehouses. It was quite a stroll from the faceless train station to that section.

The buildings here were carved straight into the rock of the Moon itself. No getting around to the back. A faded red line ran down the center of the street. At one point, automated forklifts and trucks were supposed to use that track as their guide to go between the spaceport and back.

The technology hadn't worked as it was supposed to, however, and so the red track had been abandoned.

Now, the red track had a different meaning, a play on an old Earth phrase, the red-light district. These warehouses frequently held illicit goods. It was far too easy to smuggle things to and from these buildings as they had a straight shot to the spaceport.

I would have thought that some bureaucrat in Central would have set up guards near these warehouses, to stop the illegal trade. It was probably easier (and more cost efficient) to let the trade exist and just accept bribes to look the other way.

We walked close to the buildings, right up against the walls, stopping at every door to listen.

The first warehouse wasn't our place. Not unless the crooks were making their own spaceship, given the metal grinding noises that went on behind the door.

The second through fourth warehouses were silent, with no lights.

The fifth, however, not only had lights on that we could see, I could detect the sound of men talking. Men with deep, beefy voices, to go along with their burly appearance, I expected.

Mr. Bennett agreed that this had to be the place. We couldn't sneak in through the back. However, the warehouses were built like Mr. Bennett's townhouses, and each one shared a wall with its neighbor.

What were the chances that they were connected on the inside as well?

I took a chance and stepped back, across the street, to study the buildings.

Sure enough, the one on the left, that we'd already determined was empty, looked as though it was the reflection of the one on the right, where the robbers were holed up.

The door to the empty warehouse didn't take much convincing to open. Must have been related to my office filing cabinets. Or maybe the locks were made by the same company.

This warehouse had seen better days. Instead of smelling dry and musty, the sharp smell of rat urine filled the space. The air was chilled—no one paid the heat for this place. A small group of boxes was tucked away in the far corner of the echoing room. The cardboard had been nibbled on by rats. Debris was strewn all around the bottom of the pile.

Whoever had left this property here, supposedly safe, was in for a nasty surprise when they finally came to claim it.

Not only was there a door to the other warehouse on our right, there were windows between the two spaces as well, the glass covered over with cardboard.

I knew that the door would be locked. It might even be blocked on the far side.

Instead, I walked over to the back window and carefully pried off one of the pieces of cardboard. I'd much rather have a good view of where I was going than just walking in on a surprise party.

Three men stood on the other side of the wall. They were big men, muscular. They all had flattop haircuts, the hair just starting to grow over their collars and ears, as if they'd left the Army six to eight weeks before.

Sure enough, there appeared to be a pile of gold bars to the side, next to an empty canvas bag. One of the men was working with a chemistry set, obviously melting down some of the jewelry that they'd acquired.

I stepped away from the window, tugged to the side by Mr. Bennett.

"Did you see that?" he whispered, excited. "Those are the robbers!"

I nodded. "You know that we should call the police now, right? Turn this over to them?"

Mr. Bennett sneered at me. "You think they'll drag their lazy carcasses down here at this time of night? No. The robbers will have gotten away by the time the good detectives finally make it here. We need to stop them. Now. It's our civic duty."

I didn't roll my eyes at that, no matter how much I might have wanted to.

Civic duty my ass.

"Then here's what we'll do," I told him, laying out the plan.

For once, Mr. Bennett seemed willing to follow someone else's idea.

Though I knew that before the night was over, he'd probably claim credit for all of it.

MR. BENNETT QUICKLY FOUND THINGS SIMILAR ENOUGH to rocks to throw at the front door of the other warehouse. He stayed with me until I'd loosened the cardboard on the windows closest to the robbers.

Eventually, I had my gun in one hand, and the loose cardboard in the other. I gave him a nod, then listened carefully after he left.

As soon as I heard the sharp pinging of the items Mr. Bennett threw at the door to the other warehouse, I pulled off the cardboard and shot through the glass.

The robber standing over the chemistry set went down silently. The other two were still focused on the front door. They'd already drawn their ray guns.

I shot one in the back, a good clean shot that took him down hard.

The other turned and started shooting in my direction without sighting first. The air around me sizzled.

Damn it. They had needlers. A direct shot would go straight through me, not just stun me.

I had much better sight of him than he had of me. I put him down quickly as well.

I found myself breathing heavily, as if I'd just raced up to do that shooting. I turned around, lowering my gun but keeping it in my hand.

It didn't surprise me in the least when Mr. Bennett came waltzing back in, his own gun out and aimed directly at my face.

"My dear man, it's been so lovely working with you," Mr. Bennett said as he came into the warehouse. "Unfortunately, you were unable to stop the robbers from shooting you when the time came."

"And they weren't just using stun guns, were they?" I said.

"No, they weren't," Mr. Bennett said. He chuckled. "Too bad you didn't realize that this gun has been modified into a needle ray. It will drill a hole right through you. And it will be conveniently placed in the hand of one of the killers over there."

I smiled mirthlessly, not telling him that I'd already ascertained that.

"So you were in on the robbery from the start," I said. I had thought there had been something off in his initial visit to me.

"It was my idea!" Mr. Bennett said, beaming, happy to have someone to show off to.

"Where did you meet them?" I said. I couldn't figure out where the upstanding Mr. Bennett had first been introduced to such rough men.

Mr. Bennett scowled at me. "I had some debt. It was merely a trifle. They were sent by my bookie to make sure that I was good for it."

Had Mr. Bennett been playing the ponies? Betting on rats? I'd never know, and it didn't really matter.

"I convinced them to work with me, and to rob the bank instead," Mr. Bennett said, the scorn in his voice growing. "These idiots couldn't have come up with such a plan themselves."

"Then why hire me?" I asked. I thought I knew the answer, but I wanted to make sure.

"They double-crossed me," Mr. Bennett said darkly. "After they'd committed the robbery, they were supposed to meet me so we could divvy up the goods. They never showed."

"How did you know about the red track, then?" I said.

"I knew they were staying out here someplace. I'd heard them mention it once," he said dismissively. "But I had no idea where the red track was. And I wasn't about to come out here alone."

I wondered if I'd find a complete apartment built out in the warehouse next door, or, more likely, Army sleeping bags and pillows packed away tightly into packs, ready for the next bugout.

"So you thought you'd hire me…" I prompted him.

"Yes, yes, exactly, so that you could find them for me. I've been following you ever since," Mr. Bennett said.

I could blame my headache for not noticing a tail. But the fact was, I hadn't been expecting it. I was going to have to be much more careful in the future. Particularly when it came to investigating the clients who hired me.

"You were planning this all along, weren't you? The double, or is it triple cross?" I said.

"It was why I asked if you were a religious man, on the train here," Mr. Bennett confided. "So I'd know whether or not you needed time to say your prayers before I did this."

Mr. Bennett raised the gun dramatically and fired it.

Nothing happened.

A brief look of worry crossed his face and he fired again.

Nada.

"Seems you should always check your gun, particularly after someone else has handled it," I told him, raising my own ray gun. "Or they might do something stupid like put the battery pack in upside down."

I didn't want to hear Mr. Bennett's whining anymore, so I shot him instead. I knew I only had so much time before the robbers on the other side of the warehouse woke up.

And Mr. Bennett had been right—it would take quite some time for the police to make their way out here.

TURNED OUT THAT THE CROOKS HAD BEEN dishonorably discharged from the Army. Colonel Leavenworth knew them not only by reputation but by sight. Seemed that when their source of illegal income dried up, these three had tried shaking down the Colonel, and he'd gotten them all removed from his immediate vicinity.

Let someone else take care of the problem for him instead of actually dealing with them.

Mrs. Bennett stuck by her husband, at least according to the papers. She hired the best lawyers and was in court with him every day. Didn't help, however. He was found guilty and had the book thrown at him. Seemed that Holdingbrook held grudges, and they were determined to take their pound of flesh from the man.

As for me, it didn't turn out as badly as it could have. Seemed that the robbers had already spent some of their illegally gotten gains.

I didn't take much. Just enough to cover my fee and expenses.

And possibly just a little extra, as I knew the next night alone was going to be a bad one.

I went to sleep curled around a bottle, still smelling that lily-of-the-valley perfume and dreaming of things that were never to be.

[5]

THE CASE OF THE MYSTERIOUS WIND

THERE ARE SOME THINGS THAT YOU JUST NEVER SPEND A lot of time thinking about. For example, "Why is there air?" Not unless you're a trained philosopher, which believe me, I'm not. I'm merely a private eye, hustling to make ends meet up here on the Moon, in Luna City.

The papers the last few days had been filled with reports of people complaining about strange winds blowing down the heart of downtown, following along Main Street.

Now, I'm a warren rat, born and raised on the Moon. I've never known an Earth breeze. For me, and for fellow citizens, wind is *bad*. Wind indicates a breech in the tunnel walls. It means death coming for you quickly.

Sure, Central may have clever lights hidden in the ceiling, overlapping patterns of brightness that made it seem as though you were outside on a bright sunny day. But those more open areas were only in the ritzy parts of the city. The rest of us lived in dimly lit corridors, surrounded by good solid moon rock.

Despite the winds, Central claimed there was no breach. As people weren't dying, I was inclined to believe them. It still disturbed me at a fundamental level. Central certainly didn't tell the truth about everything. For example, they still maintained that no mutants lived in the tunnels below the city, even though I, and quite a few others, knew better.

I was between cases at the moment. No one would pay me to go looking for a mysterious wind, and I wasn't desperate enough to go chasing it down on my own.

Yet.

I put in hours at my office, case or not. I kept the place professional looking, though it was my second home for me in more ways than one. For clients, I kept a water cooler burbling in the corner, a comforting sound. I had three beat-up black metal filing cabinets in the other corner, where I kept my case files—the real ones, filled with all the weirdness and what really happened, not the cleaned-up notes I sometimes handed over to lawyers or judges.

My desk stood as a barrier between me and the door on the opposite end of the room, a solid piece of faux wood that I regularly retreated behind. I kept my ray gun in one of the roomy bottom drawers. It was my philosophy that if I was any good as a private investigator, I should be able to do my job without resorting to violence, no matter how tempting it might be to smack a few heads together.

The other bottom drawer contained my biggest vice—a bottle of good whiskey.

When I was between cases, that bottle felt as though it had its own source of gravity, pulling my attention to it constantly. I'll admit there were many Fridays that I'd close up shop early just for a finger or two, only to not crawl out of the bottle until Monday morning.

What else is a fellow to do when he's married to the job, only it decides to take a vacation without him?

Fortunately, I'd only gone a couple of days between cases

at this point, when one of the weirder ones opened the door to my office.

The client didn't look odd. He looked like a fussy bureaucrat in an off-the-rack gray suit, white shirt, and muddy brown tie. His black hair was thinning—he'd be bald soon, and it wouldn't be a good look on him. Greedy black eyes peered out atop pudgy cheeks. He had a long nose, good for sticking into other people's business, and a wide mouth, probably used to order people around.

"Alvin Goodfellow?" the man inquired, giving the office a once over. "PI to the stars?" he continued, sounding incredulous.

"Best you can hire on the Moon, Venus, or Mars," I said, finishing off the jingle that I regularly ran on the radio.

Before the man could scamper off, I rose from behind my desk, automatically buttoning my suit jacket. "Won't you come in?" I said smoothly, indicating the client chairs on the far side of the desk.

He hesitated, biting his lower lip for a moment. Then he looked around again, as if making certain we were alone.

"I'd like to hire you," the man stated bluntly. "But you have to swear not to go to the police. Or the papers."

I felt myself stiffen. "I don't gossip about my clients," I told him sharply. I never had. I wasn't in it for the fame or fortune. I liked the puzzle, the putting things to right.

The man hesitated for another moment before he came to a decision. He nodded sharply, stepped into the room and shut the door firmly behind him.

"My name is James Truman. And you have to help me. My daughter's been kidnapped."

It took me a few minutes to get James settled. He seemed to collapse after his dramatic announcement, making it easy for me to lead him to a client chair and get him a glass of water.

I unbuttoned my jacket after I sat down, then pulled out a fresh notebook and turned my attention to my new client. He had the pasty white skin of a warren rat, but there was finally color returning to his pudgy cheeks. He unbuttoned his suit jacket, giving a huge sigh of relief.

Seemed he needed to get himself to a tailor and have his jacket expanded, or maybe just buy one off a different rack.

"I need to stress to you the delicate nature of this case," James said, giving my notebook a hard glare. "I work for Central."

That made me sit back and take a deep breath. "My notes are always kept in a locked desk drawer," I assured him. "When the case is finished, I keep my notes in those locked filing cabinets."

Of course, he didn't need to know that anyone with enough enthusiasm and a paperclip could break into those cabinets. The desk drawers were actually more secure, with a better lock. I didn't want anyone figuring out what I was doing during the middle of a case. I also didn't want anyone helping themselves to my whiskey. Or my ray gun.

Afterward, well, most people wouldn't believe the weird things I'd run across doing my job.

"The kidnappers told me that they'd kill Felicity if I went to the police," James continued.

"Believe me, I'm the last person who would go to the police," I told him. While there were a couple of cops who had an all right reputation, I wouldn't have called any of them *good*.

James nodded. "I'd heard that, when I asked around," he said. "That you do try to live up to your name."

I gave him a guileless smile. I'd been blessed with a babyface—big blue eyes, red hair that would curl riotously even in the dryness of the Moon, thin lips around a wide mouth, and freckles that more than one gal had assured me were cute. I used that face ruthlessly when I needed to get on someone's good side, to get information.

When I couldn't go bashing heads together.

I may not have technically always been good, as it were. But I did stay bought, if someone paid my price.

James collected himself and started laying out the facts in a cold hard voice, as if he were giving a presentation to one of his bosses about how his entire department had screwed up and he hadn't managed to pin the blame on anyone else yet.

His daughter had been taken from their home three nights before. When she hadn't come down for breakfast, his wife had gone up to her room and found a note from the kidnappers on the pillow. Beside it was hunk of Felicity's hair.

He passed the note to me. At least he'd enclosed it in a plastic envelope, so it wouldn't get torn or smudged.

The note was written in pencil, on school paper—the thick kind, with wide blue lines on it. The cursive letters had been drawn slowly, as if by a child trying to win an award for good penmanship.

> *We have Felicity. Don't go to the police or you'll start getting her back in pieces. We'll be in contact.*

"Have they been in contact?" I asked, handing the note back to him.

He gulped and nodded. "Here is where it gets tricky," he said slowly.

That sent a chill down my spine. How much money made things "tricky"?

"As I said, I work for Central, in the main air factory, east of the city, near the warehouse district." He paused, swallowed, then forced himself to continue. "The kidnappers want my passwords and my keys to the facility."

My eyebrows shot to the top of my forehead. My throat dried out and fear shot through me.

I didn't much think about where the air we breathed came from. Central provided it, along with water, lights, and the subway trains. We paid our taxes and we got the basics of life in return.

I glanced up at the ceiling, at the slowly rotating fan that was more for show than for pushing around the stale air piped in by Central.

It had never occurred to me to wonder how Central actually generated air for the warrens on the Moon. I knew it had to be made in factories, probably with huge turbines.

What would happen if some group of wackoes got hold of the air supply for the Moon? How many people would die?

For the first time in a very long time, I worried that I might be in over my head.

"How long do you have before you need to give them your information?" I asked. Might as well get all the bad news out at the start.

"Tomorrow," James said. Then his eyes darted to the side, unable to meet mine. "I've tried to put them off. But they sent me another chunk of Felicity's hair. This time, with the roots still attached." He blanched, his voice dropping to a whisper. "There was blood on it."

I found myself swallowing hard. The kidnappers had tried to be nice, just cutting off a piece of hair the first time. Tearing out a hunk wasn't the worst they could do.

Would they actually start returning her in pieces?

If they were determined enough, they might.

I had a day to solve what might be the trickiest puzzle I'd ever tackled. It certainly had the highest stakes.

I spent a few more minutes interrogating James about his daughter, her habits, his habits, where they lived, his routine, hers, anything that might give me a clue.

I can't tell you the relief I felt when I finally learned that she was in college, and not a child. The worst case scenarios had been looming, given the appearance of the ransom note.

I didn't spend time dickering over my fee. I told him what he was going to pay, and how.

Besides, it was only twice my normal rate. I knew I'd be working every minute up until the deadline.

As soon as James handed over the cash, I stood up, buttoning my jacket. "I'll accompany you to the train station," I told him.

He shook his head. "No. No! No one can see me with you! No one can know that anything is wrong."

I opened my mouth and closed it again.

Dang it. He was right.

"Fine. I'll wait here five minutes then head to the train station myself," I told him.

He swallowed nervously, then scurried out the door.

I paced behind my desk. What was James Truman not telling me? I knew there was something. Possibly several somethings.

I did believe that his daughter had been kidnapped and that she was being held against her will. I did believe that he was being blackmailed into giving desperate persons access to our most vulnerable system.

My eye fell on the newspaper still tucked away on the side of my desk.

The winds blowing down Main Street.

Were the two cases connected? Did it make sense for me to try to find out? Did I have time?

Though I'd planned on my first stop being Luna University, where Felicity had been going to school, I decided on a detour first, to go see my favorite shoeshine boy.

If anyone knew anything tangible about the errant winds in downtown Luna, Johnny would know.

Besides, if I was going to die of suffocation, might as well go out with my shoes shined.

Johnny's "throne" was empty as I came strolling up the street. He had a faux wood chair firmly attached to a solid box for his customers to sit on, so he could have better access to their shoes.

He was in his usual spot a couple of blocks off Main Street. Instead of groups of giggling girls hauling bags of shopping, the street was full of men in suits going about their serious business. Banks lined the street, along with insurance agencies, lawyers, and accountants.

In other words, well-dressed scam artists who needed to keep appearances up, as well as their shoes shined.

"Morning, boss," Johnny said as I came walking up. He wore his usual white shirt with the sleeves rolled up, showing off his muscular forearms and his dark skin. His shoulders were broad and his waist, narrow. I'd seen him haul his chair out in the mornings as if it weighed nothing.

If I were in a fist fight, I'd sure want Johnny on my side.

Over his shirt, he wore a stained gray leather apron to protect his clothes, along with nice trousers and brown Oxfords that looked brand new.

I handed him twice his usual fee for polishing up my black Oxfords. He thumbed through the bills and stuffed them away in an inside pocket, nodding.

That was one of the many smart things that Johnny did

—always insisted on payment up front, or else the fine white folk of Luna City would stiff him.

Just because Johnny's skin was the color of an unlit tunnel didn't make him stupid, despite what those idiots might think.

I knew better, and had used his keen eye to my advantage on more than one case.

In a different life, or some fantasy land where his color didn't matter, we might have even been friends.

I climbed up onto the chair, rolling up my pants legs while Johnny got out his cans of polish, brushes, and buffing cloths.

"Business has been slow this morning," Johnny admitted as he unscrewed the tin of polish.

A chemical smell rose up, like coffee that had been spiked with cheap cherry-flavored whiskey. It put me at ease, knowing that I was in the hands of a professional, despite the nasty scent.

"Why's that, do you suppose?" I asked.

Johnny shrugged as he dug his brush into the polish before he started applying it to the uppers of my shoes.

"Winds maybe chased them away?" I said, trying to sound casual.

The look Johnny shot me told me I hadn't been casual or subtle. But then he nodded and applied more polish to the sides and backs of my shoes.

"That may be. I sure wasn't the only one who was frightened and looking every direction when that first wind came along." From the shudder Johnny gave, I knew that he wasn't exaggerating.

Wind equals bad to a warren rat. Period.

"But it disappeared quickly, just blowing through town, like a sailor on leave. Breach warning bells didn't sound. Nobody was screaming, either." Johnny finished the first shoe and reached for my second.

"Was there a scent on the air? Some kind of smell?" I asked. I still wasn't sure how, or if, the two cases were related. Just a gut feeling, one that I'd learned long ago that I needed to trust.

Johnny sat back on his heels and looked up at me for a moment. "You know, there was. A sea smell. Wet," he said, nodding.

"Huh," was all I could say in response.

That sure didn't sound like a tunnel breach.

"Ever since then, there's been a run on fishbowl helmets," Johnny said, going back to his diligent work. "First couple of days, saw people hauling them around with them everywhere. But even though the wind's come back a couple of times, people have grown used to it. Strange what people will get used to."

I nodded. He was right, people did get used to things, like living underground all the times in tunnels and warrens, like fake lighting in the ceiling instead of sunlight, like distrusting winds.

Then I grinned. I had to ask. "How many times did you sell your 'personal' helmet to folks those days?"

"Why would I ever do that?" Johnny said, leaning back again so he could give me a wide-eyed, innocent look.

It didn't work for him, not like it did for me.

He grinned and shook his head. "Sold about a dozen of 'em. Three times the markup. Kept them in the box along with the polish."

I snorted. Johnny made more than I did most days, but then again, he had to deal with assholes most of the time, the good people of Luna City who didn't look past the color of his skin.

Johnny finished with the polish and started rubbing it

into the shoes with solid strokes. "Why you asking about the winds?" he said. "Got a case?"

"Maybe," I said. I knew that Johnny wouldn't talk out of turn, but I was still reluctant to say too much to him.

"You still got those helmets tucked away in your box?" I asked after Johnny had switched from the rubbing cloth to the buffing cloth, adding a high shine to my Oxfords, making them look like new.

"I do," Johnny said, nodding. He didn't look up from his work but I could tell he was listening intently.

"Keep at least one for yourself. Just in case," I said seriously.

"Got that," Johnny said. "I'll drop you a note if more of those winds come blowing around here. Deal?"

"Deal," I said.

He finished his work with a few exaggerated moves, snapping the polishing cloth loudly. "There you go, boss," he said loudly, falling back into the patter that he used with everyone else. "All clean and shining like new."

"Thank you," I told him quietly, so softly that no one else could hear. Then I fell into my own role and grunted loudly at him, stepping off the throne and walking up the street.

Yes, in a different life, we might have been friends. For now, he was just an informal informant, not someone I'd go out drinking with.

If life were different...

I WENT FROM DOWNTOWN TO THE UNIVERSITY CAMPUS —Luna U, as the locals called it—which was east of downtown, about midway between the center of the city and the warehouse district.

The buildings were all three stories tall, carved out of

moon rock then faced with tan brick. They were set up in quads, with buildings around the edges of each block and open "parks" in the center.

Narrow streets ran between the quads. In most places in Luna City, the streets were empty of vehicles. Downtown there were more, as rich people could afford taxies while the rest of us poor shmucks got around using the train or on foot.

Here, though, the streets were jammed with kids on bicycles. I'd timed my arrival perfectly wrong, as the sidewalks were crowded too—students passing between classes. It reminded me of when shift change occurred in the warrens where my office was, when empty tunnels suddenly filled with factory workers.

Fortunately, James had given me the address I needed, along with a name, Penny Hensworth, Felicity's best friend.

Penny worked as a tutor, helping poor jocks with their English papers and tests. She had set hours in the tutoring center on campus. I'd thoughtfully called ahead and booked her first slot that morning.

As I'd never gone to college, I'd never gone to any tutoring sessions. I stepped into the building and looked around eagerly, but it seemed like any regular office building, with faux wood floors, worn out gray rugs, and offices arranged in long lines along the hallways. The faint scent of young girls and their perfume lingered in the air—probably why the jocks wanted to come here in the first place. Only a few students made their way through the hallways. It was early in the semester. Once midterms arrived, students would be lined up out the door, looking for help.

No one looked twice in my direction, so I made my way up the large, concrete staircase to the second floor, then down the hallway to my meeting.

A tall, busty young woman sat behind the desk in the

tiny study room. She had brownish-red hair that fell in natural waves just past her shoulders. Her face was long and narrow, with hazel eyes that blinked at me owlishly behind thick lenses. She wore a soft gray blouse with a big bow under the neck that showed off her creamy complexion.

"Miss Hensworth?" I asked, sticking my head in.

"Yes," she said slowly. "But you're not a student," she complained.

Though I had a baby face, my days of impersonating college students were past, by at least a couple of years. "I know," I said. "And I promise not to take up too much of your time. I did sign up for your first tutoring slot for the day."

She glared at me, her disapproval evident. "I see," she said, her words frosty.

"My name's Alvin Goodfellow. Perhaps you've heard one of my ads?" I asked, humming a few bars from the jingle.

She blinked, surprised. "PI to the stars?" she asked.

The smile she gave me was like spring rousting a long, cold winter, though the edges of it were pinched, as if she wasn't used to smiling that way very often.

"That's me," I said. "I'm here on a very confidential case," I told her, taking a seat beside the table and lowering my voice.

"Really?" Miss Hensworth said, her eyes growing large.

"Really. And you can't tell anyone about it, or that I came here to see you. You think you can promise me that, Miss Hensworth?"

"Penny," she breathed out. "And I can keep a secret. I promise."

The fervent look in her eyes told me that she was telling the truth. She had secrets, secrets she might die trying to protect.

"That's swell," I told her. I handed her one of my business cards, but she didn't take it, didn't even pick it up.

"I have nosey roommates," she said. "They'd find it."

"Ah," I said, taking it back, feeling more curious than ever about the secrets this girl had.

"I need to ask you a few questions about Mrs. Polander," I said. James had mentioned this teacher as one of Felicity's favorites, who might be able to give me some insight into his daughter.

I still hadn't made up my mind for certain whether or not I would go to see her.

"Mrs. Polander teaches history," Penny said. "But you already know that. I'm taking her afternoon lectures on global development."

I nodded, as if I already knew that as well. "She primarily lectures, correct?"

"Yes, but she's always so interesting!" Penny assured me. "She doesn't just give you the facts. She tries to personalize everything, so that you'll remember."

"Have you ever gone to her office hours?" I said.

"No," Penny said, sounding offended that I would even ask such a question, the implication being that she was a good student she didn't need such a thing.

"What about the other students in the class? Do you know anyone who's gone?" I said.

Penny bit her lip, then said all in a rush, "My best friend Felicity has. But it wasn't because she wasn't doing well. She just really likes Mrs. Polander and wanted to talk to her for a while."

"I see," I said, pretending to take a note of that though I was already well aware. "Tell me about Felicity."

"She's really smart," Penny said enthusiastically. "Like, off the charts smart. And she's so committed! She really cares about everyone's well-being."

"So where would I find Felicity?" I asked, seemingly innocent enough.

Wham.

Have you ever seen those cartoons where a character's foot gets caught in a slamming door? That was what it felt like to me.

Penny Hensworth suddenly shut down. All the friendliness fled from her eyes and the frost returned.

"I wouldn't know where she is right now," she said. "You'd have to check with the registrar about her classes."

"But I thought you said she was your best friend?" I asked, confused.

Why hadn't the girl said something about Felicity being sick? Hadn't that been the excuse her parents would had given the school for her missing classes?

"We are, but we don't take the same classes, not all the time," Penny explained hastily. "Is that all?" she added, reaching for her own school books. "I could use the time to study for this afternoon's test."

I could recognize a brushoff when it slammed me in the face that way. "Thank you so much for your time," I told her, standing and buttoning my suit jacket. "Do give me a call if you think of anything else regarding Mrs. Polander. Or Felicity."

"I will," she lied. "Good day, sir."

I walked back out into the hallway, following a group of women down the stairs and out the door, onto the streets of Luna U.

What was going on here? I had believed James that his daughter had been kidnapped. Penny certainly hadn't acted as if her "best friend" wasn't in school.

Did she know about the kidnapping? Was she in on it? That was all I could think.

If I had more time, I'd spend the morning at the

university, tailing Miss Hensworth. I might still come back that afternoon, though I didn't know the girl's schedule.

In the meanwhile, I was going to try to find Mrs. Polander, hopefully catch her between classes, and see if she would give me more information about Felicity.

WHATEVER LUCK I'D HAD THAT MORNING, FIRST TALKING to Johnny then to Penny, ran out hard. I caught Mrs. Polander between classes, but she was rushing off to a faculty meeting and couldn't talk with me until later that afternoon.

This sort of lull is normal for a case, quite frankly. It was why I frequently had more than one running at the same time, so I could work one until it petered out, then switch to the other.

The only other "case" I had at the moment was the winds blowing through downtown. I'd already talked with Johnny, who was probably the best eyewitness I'd find. So I went to the secondary sources, picking up the three daily rags to see if they could illuminate the issue.

Then I took myself to a side street all-day diner. The coffee was strong enough that you had to hack off a slice to serve. They did eggs in a dozen different ways—poached, scrambled, hard-boiled, over easy, hard, or what-have-you, as well as with cheese, sausage, bacon, peppers, ham, potatoes, tomatoes, onions, and even their lunch special, which that day was thinly-sliced roast beef.

I skipped the eggs and got a biscuit that they swore was homemade (it wasn't), butter (that probably had never seen the inside of a cow), and honey (at least it was amber, though it tasted like colored Karo syrup).

I set myself up at a corner table, enjoying my repast while going through the papers. It was still only eleven AM. I figured this joint would be booked wall-to-wall come noon, so I had a bit of time.

One thing that all the sources agreed on was that the winds swept from east to west. Main Street ran north-south, so the winds blew across the street, not down it, unlike what the misleading headlines claimed.

Had the winds originated at the air factories that Central ran? They were east of downtown, after all. Had there been a breach, not in one of the tunnels, but in one of the myriad vents that Central used to pipe air into different parts of the city?

No one seemed to be investigating that aspect. All Central had to say was that they were "looking into the matter."

More than one witness had claimed that they felt as though the wind had blown off the sea. The Moon was drier than any desert on Earth. Any moisture in the air would be noticeable, particularly to those of us who'd spent our lives here.

There wasn't a centralized location for the winds, however. I didn't know if it made sense for me to go exploring some of the neighborhoods east of downtown, looking for…what? Surely Central would have admitted it if there had been a breach in one of the air vents. That would have calmed everyone down, and they'd be able to point to the repair trucks and forget the issue as it was now officially someone else's problem.

Stymied, I carefully considered my next move.

I needed to go back to the scene of the crime, as it were. Out to the townhouse owned by Mr. and Mrs. Truman. I wasn't sure what I'd find there, if anything.

But I had to do something, to keep moving on this case.

I didn't have much time, and I had the feeling I was already way behind.

THE TRUMANS LIVED IN ONE OF THE NICER neighborhoods, at the upper end of middle class. They were just a few blocks away from the truly rich folks, those who owned the banks and factories, not those who worked in them.

In the poorer neighborhoods like mine, there were apartment buildings with a single door leading to a further warrens of rooms. The next step up were town houses. They had a similar look to the apartment houses—two- or three-story buildings running the length of a block, but with several doors, each leading to an individual dwelling.

Subtle differences set the Trumans' building apart from the others. First off, the building was set further back from the street. There wasn't a yard, of course—only the very rich could afford the water it took to grow grass, trees, or even flowers. However, there was a very nice rock garden out in front of each door, with unusual boulders standing like guards. On the other blocks, all the doors looked the same. On the Trumans', color had been encouraged, so the units had at least a sliver of personality. The buildings themselves were the same, of course, carved out of solid moon rock, then faced with a different rock or brick. The Trumans' building had been faced with real brick, as far as I could tell, not the fake stuff made out of rubber.

I walked around the block, passing mothers with their strollers, a pair of old men seriously discussing the state of our society, and a couple of business men hurrying home for lunch that day. As far as I could tell, the buildings were set up in a quad, with an open space in the center for the residents to use.

As the street was mostly empty, I knew that I'd be conspicuous walking around the block a second time. I still did it, pretending to need to tie my shoelace directly across the street from the Trumans' residence.

They were the fourth door down from the corner, which had been painted a very pretty blue. (Maybe a nod to Mr. Truman's job at the Central air factory?) I couldn't tell which windows in the front belonged to Felicity, if any, or if her bedroom had faced the back of the building, the open space.

As far as I could tell, the middle section of the quad was inaccessible from the outside. You had to pass through one of the residence to get there.

How had the kidnappers taken Felicity? Had they broken into the house, drugged the girl, then carried her out the front door? That was the only thing that made sense.

Unless, of course, Felicity had left on her own. Had she been lured away? Maybe they'd gained her trust, tapped at her window, and she'd willing gone with them?

But that didn't explain the note. Not unless Felicity was complicit in her own kidnapping.

I couldn't imagine a young woman who'd voluntarily allow someone to yank out a hunk of her hair. From what I'd learned of Felicity, she wouldn't have the nerve, particularly not with that father of hers.

Still, I couldn't see how the kidnappers had, in fact, managed to kidnap her without waking anyone else in the house.

Something was very wrong with this case. And I didn't have enough clues to be able to solve it yet.

———

I WENT HOME AND CHANGED INTO A GRAY SWEATSHIRT with the spaceship logo of Luna U blazoned across the chest in purple and gold, black pants, and my softest, quietest loafers. Didn't know if it would help me fit in, but maybe someone would believe I was a mature student. Then I went back to the university.

Afternoon seemed a bit quieter on campus, with fewer students in the streets. I managed to find Penny Hensworth and followed her from one of her classes to the next. I was certain that she spotted me, though, and so wasn't about to tip her hand and go anywhere interesting.

She had secrets to keep.

I had about an hour before my meeting with Mrs. Polander at three PM. I tried to spend some time in one of the open quads. Central at least attempted to maintain the feeling of an Earth collegiate institute, and so had grass and even a few trees growing in the open space.

I tried. I really did. I sat down on the grass (which turned out to be fake) and closed my eyes, turning my face up to the bright lights in the ceiling. Many of the students were doing the same, as if I could get a suntan between classes. I made myself breathe deeply, taking the constant musty smell of the Moon into my lungs. The ground felt solid under my butt and legs. Far off in the distance I heard the chatter of students talking about their lives in very earnest voices.

However, the feeling of all that space around me kept intruding. Nobody was watching me or paying me any mind. I couldn't relax, though.

I was a warren rat. Wide open spaces bother me at a fundamental level. Give me a crowded tunnel any day of the week.

I finally gave up and went to sit in the hallway outside of Mrs. Polander's office. She came bustling up well ahead of our appointment. Her arms were full of papers, she had a rolled up set of plastic slides under one arm, and a briefcase dangled from just a couple of fingers of one hand.

"Here, let me get that for you," I offered, standing up and reaching for the door.

"Don't bother. It's locked," she said curtly. She tried shifting the pile of papers from one arm to the other. The stack nearly tipped over.

I put one hand on either side of the huge pile, gently removing it from her arms while she struggled to get her keys out of her jacket pocket.

"Thank you," she said as she got her office door open. "Why don't you just come in?"

I followed her into an office that looked as though someone had already gone through it, searching for something. Papers were strewn everywhere. Books were haphazardly stacked on the cabinets, the chairs, and even the floor. Her desk was awash with folders and more papers. An old map of the former colonies of Africa hung on the wall behind her chair, crooked, of course. Everything looked dingy and scratched up, what I could see of the desk, the chairs, and the walls.

Mrs. Polander didn't seem to think that anything was out of order, though. She walked in, placed her briefcase on her desk and slid the large collection of plastic sheets into a waiting empty circular container that looked suspiciously like a trash bin.

"Just put those anywhere," she directed as she shoved things from one side of the desk to the other, clearing a space for her to lay her briefcase down and snap it open.

There were two chairs on the other side of the desk. I let the pile slump into one of them so that the back of the chair would support the tall stack. Then I cleaned off a space for myself in the other chair, carefully placing the three books that were all intertwined onto a corner of the professor's desk.

"So, Mr. Alvin Goodfellow, PI to the stars, what could you possibly want to see an old professor of history about?"

Mrs. Polander said after she'd pulled even more papers from her briefcase and closed it.

I looked up at the severe voice. Sure, her office might be a mess and she might seem a little disorganized, but I realized right away that I was dealing with an exceedingly sharp mind.

I finally got a good look at her face, now that all that keen attention was focused on me. She had large gray eyes that gave the impression of a stormy sea just off the coast. She wore her black hair down, soft around her face. Streaks of silver and gray ran through it. Her well-plucked brows were like seagull's wings, her mouth soft and sensual, with a petite nose to anchor it all.

I would have expected her to be older, but I judged her to be about my age, in her mid to late thirties.

I knew that I should deflect her question with one of my own. Normally, I would have come up with an entire false lead, as I had with Penny.

This was a woman who'd seen all the levels of bull from students, and who wouldn't be impressed (or fooled) by my own.

"I can't tell you exactly what I'm working on," I told her earnestly. "And I can only ask that you don't repeat any of this conversation to another soul."

That at least got her attention. "Fine," she said, nodding slowly. "I will assume that you will go to the proper authorities if necessary."

"I will ma'am," I told her.

I might not have been lying.

"What can you tell me about one of your students, Felicity Truman?" I said.

Mrs. Polander sat back for a moment, thinking.

Was she trying to come up with the best lie? Or assembling everything she knew?

It appeared to be the latter, as she sat forward again and started speaking in a low, concise tone. "Felicity is a good enough student. Passionate about what catches her attention. But mercurial. Yesterday it was about helping the poor people of the Congo. Today, it's all about freeing those who are being forced to work against their will. Tomorrow, who knows?"

"I see," I said, nodding. That was along the lines of what Penny Hensworth had said as well, that Felicity cared about everything and everyone. "Tell me, would you consider Felicity to be political?"

Her father did work for Central. Had that provoked some sort of rebellion, which had led her to fall in with the wrong people?

"It's possible," Mrs. Polander said. "She has been absent the last few days. I assume she's been sick?"

"Yes, exactly," I said. "What can you tell me about her friends?"

"Her best friend is Penny Hensworth." Mrs. Polander frowned at that. "If there's anyone who's turning political, it might be her."

"What do you mean?" I asked. Penny hadn't seemed organized enough to be a threat. She should have had an easy lie already set up for me.

"She's been petitioning the university for more vegetable offerings in the cafeteria," Mrs. Polander said. "Has formed a Vegetarian Union, of all things. She has a few followers, who protest people eating meat or wearing leather."

I couldn't help but roll my eyes. Sounded as though that would be as popular as the temperance movement. All well and good on the surface, but the regular working Joe needed his or hers steak now and again.

"Who else is in this union?" I asked.

Mrs. Polander pressed her lips together in disapproval. She obviously didn't want to tell me.

"Let me rephrase that," I said. "Is there anyone in the union who you think could be a danger to either Felicity or Penny?"

"There are a couple of the boys," Mrs. Polander admitted, "who probably just joined to be with the girls, and who could be easily swayed into stupidity. Joseph Hillmander and Fredrick Smith."

"Can you think of anything else about this group, or Penny, or Felicity, that worries you? That you think you can tell me?" I said. I had two more names to research, and hopefully they'd lead me closer to Felicity.

"They're kids," Mrs. Polander said simply. "They might think they're saving the world, but they haven't really thought through the consequences. So when you find them, be sure to go easy on them. They've just made mistakes. It isn't because any of them have a bad heart."

"Got it," I said, nodding and standing. "Thank you for your time. I sure appreciate it."

Mrs. Polander sat back in her chair and peered up at me. "Whatever is going on, I hope you solve your case quickly. And feel free to come back to tell me all the details later, if you'd like. I love a good mystery."

It was only then I realized that Mrs. Polander wasn't wearing a wedding ring.

Didn't mean anything. Might just be the sort of woman who didn't wear rings.

"I will," I told her.

It might not have even been a lie.

Then I took off. I had more clues to chase down, and not much time.

THE BOYS TURNED OUT TO BE A BUST, IN SOME WAYS. They were both "sick" and hadn't been to classes for a couple of days.

However, neither of them were to be found anywhere, at their fraternity, their dorm rooms, or at their family houses.

I knew they were connected to Felicity's kidnapping. It was that gut feeling again. However, I had no idea where they were, or where they might stash a willing victim who'd possibly grown less willing.

And following Penny wasn't going to get me anywhere closer either. She'd been spooked, and it would take a couple of days for her to stop looking over her shoulder.

I didn't have a couple of days.

I headed back to my office, intending to write up the notes I had, see if I could find any other connection.

I had just sat down at my desk and was trying to string two and two together to get some kind of four when the door opened and James Truman came bursting in.

"What is it?" I asked as I stood. "What happened? Has Felicity returned?"

The hysterical laughter that James erupted with cast goosebumps all across my shoulders and spine.

"Part of her has," he finally managed to say.

He held out a small box.

Nestled inside was a single pinky finger.

"You need to go to the police," I said, sickened by my failure.

"It's too late," James said. "I've already given them my passwords and my keys."

Crap.

"We need to go stop them," I said.

"How?" James asked. His voice sounded hollow and thin.

"What sort of emergency controls are at the air factory?" I said, thinking hard.

"The usual ones?" James said, unsure what I was asking.

I wasn't completely certain what I was asking about either, just feeling my way through.

"Could you set off an alarm that would close the factory? Close off all access except to supervisors? I know you can't actually shut it down," I said. Central had started building a redundant system, but it wasn't ready yet.

They really needed to get moving on it.

"Yes," James said slowly, nodding. "Not exactly what you're asking about, but yes, something close enough. It would lock them out of the factory."

"Then let's go do that," I said. I hesitated, then took the time to pull my ray gun out of the desk. I was still in a sweatshirt, so I couldn't really wear the holster for it. Instead, I stuck into the waistband of my pants, and let the sweatshirt cover it.

"You can't shoot that inside the factory," James Truman warned as we hurried out of the office.

"We'll see," I said.

The kidnappers had just shown me how desperate they were.

We needed to be just as desperate in return.

THE AIR FACTORY WAS ABOUT MIDWAY ACROSS TOWN, between the warehouse district and Main Street. Luna City is built roughly in the shape of a large circle, with downtown in the center of things.

I don't think I'd realized just how far north the factory was located, though. It was actually on the edge of the circle, to the north.

A tall, chain-link fence topped off with barbed wire blocked the street leading to the factory. The building itself was at least five hundred yards up the street, not really clear in the dimly lit area. There were two gates in the fence, one for pedestrians and one for large construction vehicles.

Or at least that was what I assumed. You couldn't be carting air around in vans.

Alert guards were at the gate, dressed in navy jumpsuits and heavy boots, wearing hats with visors that partially obscured their faces.

I understood why. It was to make them look more intimidating. A bully was less likely to pick a fight with you if he couldn't see your eyes.

Made me want to see just how tough those goons really were.

But the guards accepted Truman's password and coded entry key and didn't even glance at me.

Hopefully after this, they'd start worrying about guests and visitors.

We hurried down the empty street. Now, I'm a warren rat. These big, empty spaces just make me nervous. It was at least three stories up to the ceiling of the tunnel, and maybe twice that wide.

The factory lurked in the distance. As we approached, I could hear the sound of the turbines, pushing the air around.

The lights grew brighter as we drew closer. The front of the building seemed like every government office building on the Moon, bland and forgettable.

What wasn't forgettable were the square vents sprouting from the rooftop, like snakes on a Medusa's head. I would have thought that solid, staid bureaucrats would have followed an engineer's concise plan, and the vents would be spaced as orderly as pickets on a fence.

Instead, they looked wild, as if each vent had been planted, then just left to grow from the rooftop to the ceiling. None of them went straight up. They veered madly from one side to the other, overlapping and twining around each other.

I didn't think it was the appropriate time to ask, but James saw my fascination and said, "It will all become clear soon. Anything you may see in the factory is strictly confidential. You don't have the security clearance for the things you're about to see. I need your word as a gentleman that you won't reveal anything. Am I clear?"

"Sure thing," I said agreeably.

What weirdness could a bunch of bureaucrats come up with, anyway?

However, this was the Moon. I should have known better.

The door to the office building was unlocked. James looked at me with worry.

"They aren't professionals," I told him. "They're probably just college students. They wouldn't think to lock the door behind them. This is actually good. It's going to make it easier, since they've been so sloppy."

"No, no it isn't," James said. He'd grown slightly pale, but hurried inside without any explanation.

I followed along, curious what had gotten my client so spooked.

Just inside the door was another security booth. It looked almost like a ticket taker's booth. It was round, like a pillar, with enough room behind the curved glass for a single guard. A large control board took up most of the space in front of the guard's chair.

Behind the chair were what looked like nets, hooks set at the end of long poles, and javelins.

What sort of security breach were they prepared to tackle?

The booth was empty. As we passed by, we found the guard, passed out cold on the floor.

He hadn't been tied up, probably just stunned with a ray gun. Again, sloppy work, as the guard could have come to at any time and raised the alarm. I knelt beside him, making sure he wasn't bleeding.

It was only then that I noticed the weird texture of the floor. It was as if someone had put down a thin coat of rubber, then, while it was still drying, sprinkled small, sharp, glittering pieces of gravel across it.

"We need to stop them. Now," James said, rushing by the guard and hurrying down the hallway.

I wasn't sure why he had such a sense of urgency, but I was inclined to agree with him, particularly since the guard didn't appear to be seriously injured.

Office doors with glass on the top half and faux wood underneath were interspersed with vents climbing the walls. At least these appeared more orderly, though again, I was surprised that there wasn't a single column of vents rising from the basement, which appeared to be where the air was being manufactured.

The sound of rushing air grew louder as we neared the back of the building. I wondered if James had just gotten so used to it that he no longer heard it. I'd never been in a tunnel breach. Few people survived those. But that was what it reminded me of, all that lovely fresh air being vented out onto the unforgiving surface of the Moon.

Another door led downstairs. The culprits hadn't bothered locking this one behind them either. Maybe they'd been worried about making a quick escape. Chances were, though, they'd just been sloppy.

The stairs leading underground were steep, though broad, and wide enough that three people could walk side-by-side down them. They were covered with the same black material as the floors in the hallway outside.

While the walls were painted beige, they, too, were

covered with the same sharp flakes of gravel. I noticed James automatically walked down the center of the staircase so he wouldn't accidentally brush against the walls.

It seemed a strange design choice for a government building.

When we reached the bottom of the stairs, James headed to the right down the first corridor, toward what looked like a bank vault door with iron bars running into the frame in all four directions, controlled by a large metal wheel in the center of the door.

At first glance, this door appeared to be locked. However, the perpetrators had merely closed it behind them.

"You can't tell anyone what you see in here," James warned again before he flung open the door.

First came the noise of a hundred fans running at high speed. Then, the rich smell of a wet, salty sea washed over me. I knew that smell, recognized it, some basic Human instinct, though I'd never been close to a sea before. Humid air came pouring out. I felt as though I was walking into the proverbial steam bath. Sweat instantly dotted my skin. It was hard to breathe with so much moisture in the air.

I stopped just inside of the door, trying to process what exactly I was seeing.

Seemed the bureaucrats at Central really did know how to get weird.

MY FIRST IMPRESSION WAS OF A WIDE-OPEN ROOM—AS big as a collegiate basketball court—filled with large silver vats, each about three feet tall. Some of them were single vats, round, and about three feet across. Others were lagoon shaped, with several vats welded together to create a larger container.

A small, four-inch control board was attached to the side of each vat, very scientific looking, with blinking lights and a dozen buttons, probably controlling the temperature in the vat, maybe providing some sort of circulation for the material inside.

The floor was covered in a much thicker coat of the gravel flakes, so sharp I could feel them through the soft soles of my loafers. The sides of each vat had received the same treatment, as had the beige walls.

Vents hung from the ceiling above the vats, noisily sucking up the air being provided by the creatures in the vats.

Because there were creatures there.

I'd never seen a live octopus, but that was what the creatures reminded me of. They had long aqua-blue tentacles that rose out of the vats. The smaller containers held smaller creatures, their arms merely three inches around.

The larger beasts had tentacles thicker than a man's thigh.

The head was a mere blob sitting at the center of those arms. Pale yellow eyes peered out balefully. Not the normal two, no, it looked as though those things had eyes that circled their entire head.

The vats they swam in were filled with a sticky green liquid that I saw trickling down the outside of some of the vats, staining the clean metal. Probably was cleaned up every day by a crew of workers sworn to silence.

Anytime one of the creatures stuck a tentacle down the side of the vat, it pulled back immediately.

Suddenly, the harsh gravel everywhere made sense. Along with the nets, hooks, and harpoons in the guard's booth.

It was to prevent these creatures from escaping.

It also might explain the crazy vents going everywhere. Instead of moving a creature as it grew from roughly three feet across to the crazy big one I saw lurking in a vat at least twenty feet across and filling the entire thing, the scientists would just attach another vat. The vents above the vats would just get added as this creature or that grew.

Someone needed to talk to Central's planning committee about this.

A graceful bubble, tinted green, floated up from one of the vats. A dozen others joined it. The bubbles were sucked up immediately by the vents above.

It took me a few moments to realize that *this* was where the air for Luna City was being generated.

These creatures were burping out the air that we needed to breathe. Huge turbines sucked it out of the room, filtered it, then pushed it out to the rest of the city.

I understood now why James had been so adamant about not talking.

Not that anyone would believe me.

Toward the back of room we caught the perpetrators, two big beefy college boys. They were struggling to remove one of the creatures from a vat. They'd brought their own container —a large, waterproof bucket with a lid.

They weren't going to poison the city's air supply.

No, much worse.

They were intent on *freeing* it.

"Stop what you're doing, you two!" James demanded as we came rushing up.

Even I had to roll my eyes at that.

Fortunately, the boys were smart enough to realize that they'd just been caught *slime*-handed, as it were. They dropped the beast they'd been trying to lift out of the vat back into its welcome home, then ran, each going a different direction.

I didn't bother chasing after either of them, but turned immediately and headed back toward the door.

There really wasn't anywhere else they could go. The room had a single entrance point.

I caught the slower one in a flying tackle, bringing him down. I wasn't trying to hurt the boy, but he still landed pretty hard on that sharp floor, cutting up his face pretty badly.

The other didn't bother to stop for his companion, but just kept running.

I stood slowly. James came racing up from behind me. "Go after him! You need to catch him!"

I nodded, winked at James, then took off at a slow jog.

I knew where the boy was going. Back to the train station.

I didn't want to spook him, or follow him too closely.

He was going to lead me back to Felicity. And unless I had this whole case figured wrong, back to Penny Hensworth as well.

THE BOY DIDN'T BOTHER LOOKING AROUND ONCE HE reached the train station. I timed it perfectly, the first time I'd managed that during this case, and got in the car behind his just before the train pulled out of the station.

The car was fairly empty, so I had a good view through the front windows at the boy. Even from that distance I could tell he was shaking, the adrenaline wearing off. He still wasn't looking around, hadn't realized that anyone was following him.

So I stood on the train, holding onto one of the metal bars that ran near the ceiling, not bothering to sit, watching to see where he'd get off and thinking about what I'd just learned.

Where had Central found those creatures? Were they from the jungles of Venus? The hidden oceans of Mars? Or perhaps the creatures had been specially bred?

I didn't think I'd ever learn the truth. Wasn't sure I even wanted to.

Had one of them broken free before? That would explain the mysterious winds blowing through downtown. Though I didn't see how one could have just escaped. Was this not the first time that someone had tried to steal one?

Or maybe someone had decided to take one home as a pet? Maybe do some experiments on it?

Either way, the creature had probably already been found by Central and returned to its proper vat. Or else we were likely to have more mysterious winds blowing through downtown.

Were they intelligent? Those eyes had seemed quite mean. But I hadn't seen a mouth that it could speak with. How did they eat?

Again, things I didn't think I needed to know.

The boy got off just before the stop for Luna U, a neighborhood that had a lot of apartment buildings and some student housing. I trailed after him by half a block.

He never looked around once.

The apartment buildings here were a step down from my own. The faux red brick was peeling off the edges of the buildings, exposing the gray moon rock beneath. As Luna City doesn't really have weather, the painted windowsills were still bright white, but the windows themselves were dirty and smudged from the inside.

A lot of students were still up, either coming back from late night study sessions or parties, or maybe both. The ubiquitous bicycles filled the street, as well as the bike racks that overflowed onto the sidewalk. I heard laughter coming from more than one brightly lit apartment, and the smell of cheap noodles cooked in garlic.

The boy walked up to the end of the street, then stopped at the door of a little corner grocery that had gone out of business. For the first time, he looked around, as if aware of his surroundings. I studiously looked away from him.

He didn't see me, appeared to think that the coast was clear, so he pulled out his keys and opened the door.

I didn't want to take the time to figure out how to break into the store. Sure, it would have a back door for deliveries. I wasn't in the mood, though, to find out what the kidnappers might do to Felicity when they discovered that the boy had come back empty-handed.

Though I hoped I wouldn't have to use it, I still drew my ray gun. Then I raced up the street as fast as I could, so I could slam into the boy's back as he opened the door.

The pair of us stumbled into the abandoned shop. I stayed pressed up against his back, slapping one hand over his mouth while pressing the tip of the ray gun to his temple.

"Listen, punk," I said quietly into his ear. "You're going to take me into the back room quietly. No grandstanding. You got it?"

He nodded frantically.

Smart boy knew that at this range, particularly to the head, even a ray gun set to stun could be deadly.

"All right. Move it," I said. I removed my hand slowly from his mouth. As he didn't cry out, I slowly moved the hand holding the gun to the middle of his back. When he stayed where he was, I pushed at him with the gun. "I said, move it."

He gulped loud enough for me to hear him, then started walking forward slowly.

Empty shelves still made corridors through the center of the shop. It smelled musty, the air stale. It was hard to see anything. However, as we progressed to the back of the shop, I saw the lighted outline of a door.

This must be where they were keeping Felicity.

I nodded, though the boy couldn't see me. He still reached for the door, opening it inward.

The pair of us stepped into the bright light. I swung my ray gun around to cover whoever else was in the room.

As I expected, Penny Hensworth was there, sitting in a chair behind a table, looking at a magazine.

What I didn't expect was that Felicity sat beside her, giggling.

IT SEEMED THAT FELICITY HAD BEEN "IN" ON THE kidnapping from the start so that they could get hold of one of the creatures who manufactured the air for Luna City.

Kids these days. They really needed to find a different crime than pretending to be kidnapped.

As the phone in the shop still worked, I called James to let him know where we were, and that his daughter was safe.

She was whole, too. Seemed that finger had been a clever fake.

James Truman arrived almost immediately after that with four of the security guards from Central, the ones who wore gray visors down over their eyes.

It was interesting how neither father nor daughter said a word to each other, though I could tell that James was relieved to see her.

James seemed resigned as the guards escorted the boy and the two girls away.

"What's going to happen to them?" I asked after they'd left.

James shrugged.

"They're just kids. Stupid, sure. But not necessarily bad apples," I told him, repeating what Mrs. Polander had said.

"Even Penny Hensworth?" he said sharply.

I hesitated. While we were waiting, she'd gone on and on about how it was cruel to make those creatures work for us, how they needed to be freed.

Did they though? Even Penny finally admitted as I sat there that they weren't intelligent. They had no consciousness, not like Humans, or Venusians, or even the warriors from Mars.

"Probably," I said. "Though Central may want to keep an eye on her."

James nodded. He cleared his throat, wanting to say something more.

I just stood there, waiting.

"About what you saw," he started.

I snorted. "Who would believe me?"

I mean, really, monstrous sea-like creatures who generated all the air for the people on the Moon?

James gave me a sad smile. "Exactly," he said. "You're a good man," he added after a few moments.

"It's in the name," I said, also part of the ad jingle, though not as memorable as being the PI to the stars.

James walked me to the train station. I knew that I'd have a tail for the next couple of weeks. Depending on the cases that came my way, that might or might not be a good thing.

I had solved the case of the kidnapped daughter as well as the mysterious wind, not that I would ever tell a soul. It was early still, not yet seven PM. I wasn't sure what I was going to do next.

I didn't want to go back to my lonely, one-room apartment. I could already hear the bottle of whiskey calling to me.

The air provided to the citizens of Luna City was safe. Nothing to worry about. But I still felt as though it had been a near miss.

What had the kids planned on doing with the creature

once they had it in their possession? Had Penny planned on contacting the press? Did she not realize that they, too, were owned by Central?

Ah, to be so young and so naïve.

I kept feeling that wind on my face as I rode the train back to my neighborhood. I had nowhere else to go. No friends, not really.

If Central decided to make me disappear, no one would really notice, particularly not dear old Mom sitting in the old folks' home.

As I slowly made my way from the station toward my apartment building, I heard the sound of live music in the air.

I wasn't much of an aficionado, so I didn't go seeking out that sort of thing.

But tonight, I just felt the need of some company.

I turned toward the elusive notes, only to find that they were coming out of the local community center.

Seemed there was a dance lesson going on that night.

I hadn't noticed any lack of speed when I'd been chasing after those teenagers. But it wouldn't do for me to get out of shape, either.

After all, shouldn't the PI to the stars know how to dance?

ABOUT THE AUTHOR

Leah Cutter writes page-turning fiction in exotic locations, such as a magical New Orleans, the ancient Orient, Hungary, the Oregon coast, rural Kentucky, Seattle, Minneapolis, and many others.

She writes literary, fantasy, mystery, science fiction, and horror fiction. Her short fiction has been published in magazines like *Alfred Hitchcock's Mystery Magazine* and *Talebones*, anthologies like Fiction River, and on the web. Her long fiction has been published both by New York publishers as well as small presses.

Find Leah's books on Knotted Road Press at (www.KnottedRoadPress.com)

Follow her blog at www.LeahCutter.com.

Reviews

It's true. Reviews help me sell more books. If you've enjoyed this story, please consider leaving a review of it on your favorite site.

Come someplace new...

Are you a traveler? Do you enjoy exploring strange new worlds, new cultures, new people?

Journey into the various lands envisioned by Leah Cutter.

Sign up for my newsletter and I'll start you on your travels with a free copy of my book, *The Island Sampler*.

I will never spam you or use your email for nefarious purposes. You can also unsubscribe at any time.

http://www.LeahCutter.com/newsletter/

ABOUT KNOTTED ROAD PRESS

Knotted Road Press fiction specializes in dynamic writing set in mysterious, exotic locations.

Knotted Road Press non-fiction publishes autobiographies, business books, cookbooks, and how-to books with unique voices.

Knotted Road Press creates DRM-free ebooks as well as high-quality print books for readers around the world.

With authors in a variety of genres including literary, poetry, mystery, fantasy, and science fiction, Knotted Road Press has something for everyone.

Knotted Road Press
www.KnottedRoadPress.com